THE WISH-FULFILLING COW
and Other Classic Indian Tales

Author, poet and translator, Deepa Agarwal, writes for both children and adults and has written over 50 books. A frequent contributor to magazines and journals in India and abroad, she has edited and compiled several anthologies. Among other awards, she has received the N.C.E.R.T. National Award for Children's Literature in 1993 for her picture book *Ashok's New Friends*, while her historical fiction *Caravan to Tibet* was on the IBBY (International Board on Books for Young People) Honour List 2008. Her work has been translated into several Indian and foreign languages. Recent titles include *The Game of Shadows* (Scholastic India) and *Chanakya, the Master of Statecraft* (Penguin India). She also researches children's literature, actively promotes reading and conducts creative writing workshops and storytelling sessions.

The Wish-fulfilling Cow and Other Classic Indian Tales

Deepa Agarwal

Illustrations by Siddharth Ghosh

SCHOLASTIC
New York Toronto London Auckland
Sydney New Delhi Hong Kong

For Adya, Kartik, Aanya, Anika and Ahan

The Tale of the Ring and *The Silent Queen* have appeared in *Cricket* magazine, under the title *The Mute Queen*.

Published by Scholastic India Pvt. Ltd.
A subsidiary of Scholastic Inc., New York, 10012 (USA)
Publishers since 1920, with international operations in Canada, Australia, New Zealand, the United Kingdom, India, and Hong Kong.

For information regarding permission, write to:
Scholastic India Pvt. Ltd.
A-27, Ground Floor, Bharti Sigma Centre
Infocity-1, Sector 34, Gurgaon 122001 (India)

Designed and typeset by Ram Das Lal

First edition: January 2015
This reprint edition: September 2025

ISBN-13: 978-93-5103-707-1

Printed at Shiv Shakti Printing and Trading Co., Haryana

Contents

A Feast for Ganesh!

Kuber, the god of wealth, was also the treasurer of the gods and had access to all the riches of the earth. As king of the Yakshas, he ruled the fabulous city of Alakapuri, which rivalled Indra's capital in splendour. Since he was deformed and found it hard to get around on his own, Vishwakarma, the architect of the gods, had created a special chariot for him that could fly everywhere. It was large enough to carry a whole city! Kuber was extremely proud of his possessions and believed he was superior to the other gods. He lost no opportunity to flaunt his riches to belittle others.

Shiva, on the other hand, was an absolute contrast to Kuber. He led a frugal existence on Mount Kailash and had no desire for fine clothes, jewels and luxuries. His followers, too, were ascetics like him.

Kuber did not think much of Shiva for living so humbly

and just could not stomach the fact that the other gods respected Shiva more than him. He was also envious that so many humans worshipped Shiva. So overcome was he by envy that he decided he would prove to Shiva once and for all that he was the greater of the two.

So Kuber hatched a plan and set off for Shiva's abode on his fabulous chariot. Shiva received him with his usual courtesy and asked him what had brought him to Mount Kailash.

'Most respected Lord Mahadev,' Kuber said, 'I have come for a special purpose—to invite you to my humble abode. I have long wanted to throw a feast in your honour and have already sent out invitations to all the gods. It will be a great privilege if you attend. Please be kind enough to oblige me with your presence.'

Shiva guessed what Kuber was up to. He smiled and said, 'I am touched by your sentiments, dear Kuber. But it is not possible for me to come to your feast. However, since you have already invited many guests, if you don't mind, I will send my son Ganesh to represent me instead. But there is one thing I must mention—he has an enormous appetite and it is next to impossible to satisfy it. In fact, if you have the slightest misgivings about this, I would suggest you take back your invitation.'

For Kuber, this was like an open challenge. He replied, 'How I wish you would have been able to attend, Lord! But I will be more than happy to welcome your dear son.' Then he laughed, 'As for his being a big eater, I can assure you that I will be equal to the task of providing adequate food. If I, the god of wealth, am incapable of satisfying a little child's appetite, of what use are all my treasures?'

Shiva smiled mysteriously once more. 'Alright,' he said, 'take the boy with you. But remember, I have warned you.'

'You will have your joke, Lord,' Kuber laughed. 'And now, as soon as Ganesh is ready, I will take my leave.'

Kuber flew off with Shiva's son to his magnificent city. The yakshas were amused to see the small guest who was dressed in such ordinary clothes. But giving him due respect, they welcomed him with folded hands. As soon as they entered his gorgeous palace with its gleaming marble floors, gold and jewel-studded pillars and silken hangings, Kuber summoned his attendants.

'Get the ceremonial bath ready,' he said. 'Bring the most fragrant oils and perfumes for my guest and the most expensive clothes, so he is suitably dressed for the feast.' Ganesh was given a long and luxurious bath. After that the attendants decked him in garments of the finest silk, bordered with gold and embroidered with pearls and rubies, and hung fabulous jewels around his neck and in his ears.

Then Ganesh was led to the grand banquet hall where plates and glasses of solid gold had been laid out for the guests. Garlands of fragrant flowers ornamented the hall and divine performers played melodious music. After the invocations to the gods had been made, the delicacies began to arrive. Ganesh began to savour each and every dish with great relish. Kuber served his honoured guest himself, saying, 'Ganeshji, try this delicately flavoured dish. And here's another crisp puri for you. Your father said you have a good appetite. You must satisfy it fully.' As he played the gracious host, he kept thinking, Lord Shiva is really fond of joking. How much can this little child eat?

But after a while, Kubera's arms began to ache, putting food in the child's plate, and he decided to let his attendants take over the job. He also began to get a little worried. No matter how quickly Ganesh's thali was refilled, he managed to empty it in a trice!

Worse, he would immediately cry, 'I'm still hungry! Bring more food!' More food had to be piled onto his plate at once. The servants became so busy serving him that they could not take care of the other guests. In any case, all the others had stopped eating to watch Ganesh with wide-eyed amusement. They watched him polish off enormous platters of modak, laddoos and pedas and wash it all down with large jugs of buttermilk, then gobble up huge bowls of kheer at breakneck speed.

Watching this, Kuber became increasingly anxious. Maybe Shiva had not been joking; maybe he was actually

serious when he said that his son had an insatiable appetite. Kuber began to sweat so much that his silk garments were soaked through and through. The sight of Ganesh devouring everything in sight turned him dizzy. Worse, the child kept waving his hands, demanding more and more.

'Tell the cooks to prepare more food!' Kuber shouted at the attendants, almost tearing off his necklace of enormous diamonds in frustration. 'This child cannot go home hungry!'

There was utter pandemonium in the kitchen. The cooks rushed to and fro—chopping, grinding, mixing, kneading, stirring and frying. They were so tired that they could barely stand. Some were beginning to keel over from exhaustion, others were trying to sneak away, terrified at what was happening!

The head of Kubera's household came to him in panic. 'Your majesty, the... the cooks have collapsed,' he whispered in Kubera's ear. 'And... and ... there is nothing left to cook! We have emptied out all the stores.'

'How is that possible?' Kuber screamed. 'How can my larder get empty? I am the god of wealth. Go, buy some more provisions!'

'Bring me something to eat,' Ganesh was shouting. 'Quickly! I'm still hungry! I can't wait! I'm so hungry I can eat anything. Don't you have any more food? Alright ... maybe I'll try this gold plate. It looks very valuable.

It should taste good.' He took a bite of the plate and crunched it up within seconds.

Kuber almost fainted when he saw all his plates, the jewel-studded glasses, the golden chairs and his fabulous chandeliers vanish into Ganesh's mouth.

He fell to the ground, prostrating himself before the insatiable child and said, 'I beg you, Lord Ganesh, have pity on me. Please spare my palace!'

'But I am still ravenous. If I don't get more food, I will have to gobble you up too!' Ganesh said, eyeing Kuber hungrily.

Kuber realised that he was on the brink of ruin. The whole of his magnificent kingdom was about to vanish. What was he to do? Who could he ask for help? His heart sank as he thought, 'Who else but Shiva?' He had no choice but to appeal to Ganesh's father, the very god he was trying to belittle.

The god of wealth leapt into his chariot, dashed to Mount Kailash and flung himself at Shiva's feet. 'Forgive me for my arrogance, Lord!' he pleaded. 'You warned me, but I was blinded by pride and I underestimated your son. All the sumptuous delicacies I served were not sufficient to fill Ganesh's belly. He has consumed all the food in Alakapuri, and is now devouring my palace. Please, I beg you, save me! I will never boast about my riches again.'

Shiva smiled again and asked Parvati for a handful of roasted rice. 'Give this to him,' he said. 'The simplest food offered with love will be more than a feast for Ganesh. It will satisfy his hunger at once.'

By the time Kuber returned, almost the whole of the fabulous city of Alakapuri was in Ganesh's belly. And the little god had acquired an enormous paunch!

Kuber went down on his knees and said, 'Dear Ganeshji, I may be the god of wealth, the guardian of all the treasures of the earth, but this is all the food I have left now. I offer it to you with love and utmost humility. Please accept it.'

Ganesh tossed the handful of rice into his mouth and stroked his tummy. Then, letting out a large burp, he said, 'Now I am quite full.'

Ever since then Ganesh has had a large belly. As for Kuber, he became an ardent devotee of Lord Shiva and was the recipient of many of his favours in due course.

A Mother's Ransom

The great sage Kashyap had two wives, Kadru and Vinata, both daughters of Prajapati Daksha. Kadru had lost an eye, which marred her appearance. Vinata, on the other hand, was charming to look at. The two sisters were bitter rivals.

Neither of them gave birth to any children. This troubled Kashyap a great deal as he was keen to have a son. So he decided to perform a rite that would make it possible. Since he was highly respected, all the gods, Gandharvas and sages came to his aid. Indra too was asked to gather wood to burn in the ceremony. Being all-powerful, Indra was able to fetch a mountain of wood in the blink of an eye. On his way back, he happened to notice the Valakhilyas, a group of tiny ascetics as small as a thumb, carrying one stalk of palash for the ritual, together. Unfortunately, they had got trapped in a cow's water-filled footprint, and were struggling to get out.

Indra was most amused and began to laugh at the sight. And instead of helping them, he mocked them and went off without paying his respects. The holy men were enraged. To teach the arrogant god a lesson, they prayed to Agni to create another king of the heavens, someone who would be much stronger than Indra.

When this word got to Indra's ears, he realised that he had made a grave mistake. Terrified at the thought of being dethroned, he appealed to sage Kashyap for help. Kashyap agreed to smooth things over. He went to the Valakhilyas and told them that since Indra had been appointed by Brahma as the king of the three worlds, their prayer showed disrespect to the creator. They should ask for a king of the birds instead.

The tiny hermits said, 'We will go by your advice, holy sage. But we want the arrogant king of the heavens to be humbled. You desire a son. Let us ask Agni for a son for you who will be powerful enough to defeat Indra but will not dethrone him.'

'That's an excellent idea,' Kashyap replied.

The fire sacrifice was performed to Kashyap's satisfaction. Kadru and Vinata too completed the fasts and prayers required of them and went to Kashyap to ask for a boon. Kadru made her request first. She asked for a thousand sons. Hearing this, Vinata immediately felt insecure and entreated her husband to give her two sons who would be stronger than Kadru's thousand. He blessed her, saying she would have two brave sons who would be overlords of all the birds.

Kashyap gave Vinata the seed for them, the way he had given it to Kadru.

The two wives placed their eggs in warmed jars. Five hundred years passed. Kadru's sons, the Nagas or snakes, came crawling out of the jar, a thousand of them.

Vinata's sons, however, did not appear. Anxious and impatient, she broke one of the two eggs. But the moment she set eyes on her newborn son, Vinata cried out in dismay. Only the top part of his body was properly formed! Worse still, the son, Aruna, was furious with his mother for forcing this premature birth.

'Could you not wait until I was fully grown? I am now doomed to be misshapen, mother. For this reason, I lay this curse upon you! You will become a slave to your co-wife, Kadru!' he cried.

'My son, how can you condemn your mother to this fate?' Vinata cried, horrified. 'I did it only because I was desperate to set eyes on you. You have cursed me to a life of utter misery. You know how much your stepmother hates me.'

Aruna's anger was beginning to cool down a little. 'I cannot take back my curse,' he said. 'However, I can offer a remedy. Your second son Garuda will set you free. But please wait for him to be born naturally so he emerges in complete shape and full of power.'

Saying this, he flew into the sky where he became the charioteer of the sun.

Vinata resigned herself to waiting for her second son's birth. One day, she and Kadru were walking by the side of the sea when the celestial horse Ucchasravas (who had emerged from the ocean when it was churned for nectar) came galloping by.

'What colour is that horse?' Kadru asked.

'White,' Vinata replied immediately.

'But his tail is black,' Kadru insisted.

'No,' Vinata replied. 'That's not correct. He is white all over, white as milk.'

Kadru laid a bet with Vinata, saying, 'Whoever is wrong about the colour of the tail will agree to be the other's slave.'

'Agreed,' Vinata said immediately. 'But you're going to lose. I know he's completely white.'

'Don't be so sure,' Kadru sneered. 'Let us go to his abode and see who's right.'

Kadru had actually concocted a scheme to trap Vinata. She commanded her sons, the serpents, to turn into black hair and cover Ucchasravas's white tail completely. To her surprise, many of them refused to be part of her deceit. Furious, Kadru cursed them, 'You have dared to disobey your mother! For this impertinence, I place a curse upon you. You will all be consumed in a sacrificial fire.'

These were the serpents that were later consumed in the fire of Janamejaya's yagya during which the story of the *Mahabharata* was first told.

Terrified, the rest of her sons agreed to do her bidding. The next morning when the two sisters went to examine the horse again, Vinata was shocked to find that Ucchasravas's tail had turned black!

'What did I tell you?' Kadru was triumphant.

Poor Vinata did not know what to say! She knew that Kadru had tricked her. But since she had agreed to the bet, she was forced to serve as her sister's slave now.

Five hundred years passed and Garuda broke out of his egg.

As soon as he was born, he began to grow, and in no time, expanded to an immense size. His voice was so loud that his call shook the sky. Garuda looked around for his mother and on not finding her, flew out in search of her. His huge wings shone like gold and when he flapped them against the wind, the sound was alarmingly loud. As he soared higher, he came close to the abode of the gods. His wings gleamed so bright that their lustre blinded the devas.

The celestial ones were thrown into a panic. They thought he was a huge mass of flames coming to devour them. They ran to Agni.

'What is this new fire that is as dazzling as you, Agni? Indra asked.

'It is Garuda,' Agni said. 'He is the son of sage Kashyap and Vinata. His father had granted a boon to his mother that she would have a son who would be equal to Indra in power. His power and brilliance is equal to mine.'

Indra's equal? The gods were extremely troubled to hear this. What if Kashyap's son decided to challenge the king of the heavens?

To win Garuda over, they decided to approach him singing songs of praise. 'O great son of Kashyap,' they said, 'your glory is greater than that of Agni. Please dim your radiance so that it doesn't blind us.'

Hearing them, Garuda reduced his brightness a thousandfold so the gods would be able to see clearly.

At that time he had no intention of matching his might against Indra. All he wanted to do was find his mother. Garuda flew all over and discovered his mother on the other side of the ocean where he was born.

When she set eyes on her son, Vinata was overjoyed.

She had been leading a wretched life as Kadru's slave. Her sister constantly ordered her around and made her labour over the most difficult tasks.

They had barely exchanged greetings when Garuda heard Kadru call out, commanding his mother to carry her and her sons to an island that might be more suitable for them. 'My son, I am sorry to inform you that you have been born into slavery,' Vinata wept. 'You will have to do my sister's bidding too.'

'Never mind, mother,' Garuda said. 'At least I can lighten your burden.'

He picked up the serpents on his back and winged off. But he flew so high that they came too close to the sun. Affected by its heat, the snakes began to faint. Kadru, who was on Vinata's back, saw her sons suffering and prayed to Indra. The god was pleased and sent dark clouds to cover the sun and showers of rain that cooled the serpents.

The party finally reached the beautiful island of Ramanayika. It was full of verdant trees and cool streams. But the snakes were not satisfied and wanted to try some other place.

'Take us to a better island,' they said. 'You fly all over the sky, O Garuda. You must know which place is the best.'

Garuda did not like being ordered about by his half-brothers. He asked his mother why he was expected to do whatever they asked.

Vinata told him the whole story, how Kadru had tricked her and made her a slave. 'Your older brother predicted that you will set me free,' she said.

Garuda was furious when he heard how his mother had been duped. 'I will use all the power I possess to release you, mother,' he said.

He went to Kadru right away and asked her what he

could do to release his mother from this bondage. Kadru had no desire to lose her slave. She thought fast and came up with a task that she knew was impossible for anyone to accomplish. 'Bring me some amrit, the immortal nectar of the gods, and I will let your mother go,' she said.

'Where can I find this amrit?' Garuda asked Vinata.

'You will find it in the heavens, son,' Vinata said with a sigh. 'But it is an extremely challenging task, for Indra and the other gods guard it carefully from the asuras and rakshasas who are always trying to steal it.'

'I will find a way,' Garuda said.

He spread his enormous wings and flew off. After a while he began to get hungry and started searching for something to eat. He came across an elephant and a tortoise fighting on the banks of a lake. Garuda swooped down and picked them up in his claws, thinking they would make a good meal. The animals were actually two sages—brothers who had quarrelled and cursed each other to turn into animals. They continued to fight in their next form as well.

Now, Garuda wanted to find a place where he could eat his meal in peace. He reached a spot that was sacred. But the breeze from his great wings was so strong that it made the divine trees tremble. Only the huge Rauhina tree offered him a branch to sit on. Once his hunger was satisfied, Garuda set off to find the amrit so he could free his mother. Unknown to him, as he came closer to the heavens, the most ominous events were taking place. The gods began to notice that the celestial garlands in their palaces were losing their fragrance and a pall of dust was beginning to settle on everything. Meteors and comets began to shoot through the skies and the gods realised that some calamity was about to break upon them.

Alarmed by these omens, Indra hurried to Brihaspati, the guru of the gods, and asked for his advice. 'Lord of the heavens, this is the consequence of your pride,' the sage said. 'You mocked the Valakhilyas, and they cursed you, asking Agni to create a being who could humble you. As a result, the mighty son of Kashyap was born. Now he is coming to take the immortal nectar away. Do not underestimate him; he is no ordinary enemy who can be easily defeated. He is equal to you in power and can assume any shape he desires.'

When they heard this, the gods doubled their vigilance and Indra himself stood guard with his mighty thunderbolt, protecting the amrit. But Garuda proved more than a match for the celestial army. To Indra's dismay, his thunderbolt simply glanced off Garuda's feathers when he hurled it. Very soon, the devas were forced to retreat and beg the five elements—Prithvi, Agni, Jal, Vayu and Akash—to help them. However, even the combined might of all the gods and the five elements could not prevail over Garuda. He countered

Vayu's whirlwind with a stronger one. His mighty wings wreaked such havoc that the celestial powers fled in terror. After routing the gods, Garuda headed for the place where the divine nectar was stored. He found it was protected by many barriers that were almost insurmountable.

First of all, Garuda had to break through an enormous ring of fire whose flames soared to the highest point in the skies. He had to do it fast since the gods were likely to regroup and attack him. He quickly multiplied the number of mouths. Ninety times ninety mouths drank up all the rivers of the earth. He poured this ocean of water on the fire and put it out.

The next obstacle was no less daunting. The gods had created the vighna yantra to protect the amrit—a huge iron wheel with a thousand sharp blades that rotated constantly at great speed. Calculating the distance between these blades, Garuda reduced himself to a tiny size, and propelling himself with immense force, darted between them in the flash of an eye. But the nectar was still beyond his reach, for two great serpents were coiled beneath the wheel. Their eyes, which never blinked, could reduce whoever they looked upon to ashes, with just a glance. Garuda created a whirlwind that flung dust into their eyes. And finally, he seized the pot of nectar, uprooted the wheel and flew off.

However, Garuda made no attempt to drink the

nectar as the gods had expected and feared. As Garuda passed him in his flight, Lord Vishnu also noted this. 'You are truly a noble creature,' he said. 'You have employed all your strength to lay hands on the precious amrit but are not using it to make yourself immortal. As a reward, I would like to gift you a boon.'

Garuda asked, 'Grant that I will always fly above you, Lord, and escape old age and death without drinking the nectar of immortality.'

'So be it!' Vishnu proclaimed.

In turn, Garuda also offered the god a boon. When Vishnu said that he wished to make Garuda his vehicle, Garuda agreed readily. The god placed Garuda's likeness on his banner; in this manner, he was always above him.

But how could Indra let Garuda get away with the nectar? He hurtled after Garuda and flung his powerful thunderbolt at him again. Garuda simply smiled. 'I pay my respects to the noble sage Dadhichi from whose bones your vajra has been created,' he said, bowing his head, 'and honour your great strength as well, O Lord of the Heavens.' As he spoke, he let one of his feathers loose into the air so that the sage and the invincible weapon of Indra would not be shamed.

Impressed by his generosity of spirit, Indra caught the feather and said, 'Dear Garuda, I wish to be your friend. But I would like you to tell me the extent of your strength.'

Garuda replied, 'I will be deeply honoured and happy too, to be your friend. I will also let you know how strong I am, although it is not proper to praise one's own self. Noble Indra, I can carry all three worlds on one wing, along with you, without any effort.'

Indra was awestruck. 'Then I have no reason to be humiliated by this defeat,' he said. 'But tell me one thing, great bird, why are you taking this nectar?'

Garuda replied, 'My stepmother Kadru trapped my mother into slavery and as soon as I was born I too was forced to serve her and her sons. I asked Kadru what she wanted in order to set us free. She said that she wanted me to bring her amrit as our ransom.'

'You can deliver the amrit to the snakes, but only the devas are permitted to taste it,' Indra said. 'Leave it on the island. I'll take care of the rest.'

'As you say, O king of the heavens,' Garuda replied.

Indra was very pleased to hear this. 'You deserve a boon for your noble actions,' he said. 'Ask what you will.'

Remembering how the serpents had deceived his mother, Garuda said, 'The serpents are my born enemies. Let them always be my prey. And ... I also desire to study the Vedas.'

'So be it,' Indra replied.

Garuda landed on the island of the Nagas. Kadru was dumbfounded when she saw him appear bearing the pot of amrit.

'I have brought the divine nectar as you requested,' Garuda told her. 'Now fulfil your promise and let my mother go. One more thing, the serpents should take a purifying bath before touching the amrit.'

Overjoyed that her sons would be able to achieve immortality and be equal to the gods, Kadru agreed at once.

'Vinata is no longer my slave. You have redeemed her,' she said.

Garuda placed the pot of amrit on a clump of durva grass with great care. Indra reduced himself to the size of an ant and hid beneath the pot. Then Garuda took his mother on his back and flew away with her as far as he could from the isle of the Nagas.

Kadru told her sons to go and purify themselves. In the meantime, Indra returned to his normal size, snatched the pot away and made for his heavenly abode.

The serpents returned from their bath. Even though they saw that the pot of amrit was gone, they licked the place where it had been kept, hoping to find some drops that might have spilled over. The sharp grass split their tongues and from that day, snakes have forked tongues. The durva grass on which the amrit was placed is considered holy since then and is used in worship to this day.

Garuda carried his mother over the oceans and found a suitable place for her to live in. Then he returned to the Rauhina tree to study the Vedas. He reigned over the birds and other flying creatures while Indra ruled the rest of the heavens, and they always remained friends. Garuda also became the vehicle of Lord Vishnu as he had desired.

The Wish-fulfilling Cow

Sage Vashishth, like the other Saptarishis or seven holy sages, led a simple life in his forest hermitage. As a teacher, he imparted knowledge of the scriptures as well as other forms of learning to his disciples. Apart from their studies, the residents of the ashram spent their time in prayer and meditation. Since they had chosen to be ascetics, the pleasures and luxuries ordinary people craved for did not hold much attraction for them. They wore the simplest of clothing and lived on fruit, edible roots and berries, which they gathered from the forest. And if ever the sage needed something beyond this, he could acquire it quite easily.

This was because he possessed the holy wish-fulfilling cow, Kamadhenu. Kamadhenu had a beautiful calf called Nandini who also had this power. Kamadhenu, also known as Surabhi, meaning the fragrant one, was indeed very special. She was one of the sacred beings that had emerged at the time of the churning of the ocean, the Samudramanthan, when the gods and asuras were trying to extract the immortal nectar—amrit—from the ocean. Brahma had gifted her to the sages so that they could have a constant supply of milk and ghee for their rituals.

King Vishwamitra ruled a kingdom close to the forest where Vashishth lived. The sage's fame had spread to this kingdom too. People revered him for his learning, and often talked about the remarkable powers that he had acquired through his rigorous tapasyas. All this talk reached the king's ears and Vishwamitra began to get jealous of his subjects' reverence towards Rishi Vashishth. He felt that as the king, he should command more respect. How could a sage who lived a humble life in the forest be placed on a higher pedestal than a monarch?

One day he decided to go to the forest and find out for himself what was so special about Vashishth. He took his army with him to make it clear to the sage that real authority lay with him, the ruler of the area.

Vashishth welcomed Vishwamitra with all the honour due to a guest. He offered him and his entourage the best of what was available at the hermitage. But after a while the sage's disciples came and whispered in his ear, 'What shall we do, Guruji? The king has a whole army with him. The laws of hospitality demand that we offer them food.

But from where can we get enough to feed them all?'

'Do not worry,' said the sage, unruffled. 'There will be enough food for everyone.' He had guessed that the king had deliberately come to test his powers. But Vashishth was more than equal to the challenge.

Excusing himself, he went out and addressed Kamadhenu. 'Revered goddess, my reputation as a host is at stake. I appeal to your benevolence.'

Kamadhenu lowered her head gently. 'Do not worry, honourable rishi. I will supply whatever you need,' she replied.

Vashishth called his disciples. 'I will attend to his majesty,' he said.

'You go and request the king's army to be seated and lay out the leaf plates.'

'But Guruji, where's the food?' The disciples wrung their hands.

'Here it is,' said the sage, waving his hand.

His students were wonder-struck. A most wonderful aroma filled the air. As they watched, wide-eyed, rows of delicious dishes appeared ... the choicest variety of vegetables, rice, breads, fruit and sweets they had ever seen. It was a banquet they could never have imagined possible! And it had appeared magically, from nowhere. Where had their guru produced so much food from right in the middle of the forest? But they knew better than to ask questions. They ran to summon their guests.

Vishwamitra frowned in disbelief when he saw the lavish spread laid out. His army was already feasting to their heart's content. But even as he sat to eat, one thought kept troubling him. How had the sage produced this banquet in the middle of nowhere? Did he really have such extraordinary powers? It would have been a challenge for him, as a king, living in the city, with immense resources at his command to feed an army at such short notice. How could a sage who barely owned anything offer such a repast to his guests?

Finally the king could not control himself any longer. As he was leaving, he said, 'I thank you immensely for your hospitality, O sage. It exceeded all bounds. We could never have dreamt of getting such a sumptuous meal in this wilderness at such short notice. You did not even know that I was coming, and such delicacies are not to be found here in the forest. How did you manage it?'

The sage smiled. 'We may be ascetics and live simply in the forest,' he said, 'but we have resources too, O king.'

The king frowned. 'Obviously you have your resources. But it appears that you wish to keep them secret.'

'No, king. It is not a secret,' Vashishth replied. 'The sacred wish-fulfilling cow Kamadhenu provides me with anything in the world I ask for.'

The king's eyes opened wide with surprise. The wish-fulfilling cow! No wonder the sage could produce a banquet in a trice. A pang of jealousy shot through him. Why should this hermit possess something as extraordinary as a wish-fulfilling cow when he, the king, did not have anything to match it?

'The wondrous Kamadhenu? Can I pay my respects to her?' he asked. Already a plan was being formed in his mind.

'As you wish, O king,' Vashishth replied. 'Follow me!'

The rishi led the king to Kamadhenu, though he had guessed what thoughts were coursing through Vishwamitra's mind. And when the king set eyes upon Kamadhenu, the desire to own this extraordinary being increased a hundred-fold.

'Noble rishi, I have a request,' Vishwamitra said.

'O mighty king, what kind of request do you wish to make to a humble ascetic?' Vashishth asked.

'Rightly said,' replied the king at once. 'You are an ascetic. You have renounced luxuries.' He pointed to Kamadhenu. 'Why do you need this magical cow? Give her to me. I am the king! It is more suitable that she add to the glory of the royal cowsheds. There she will be pampered and receive the best of fodder and care as befits her.'

'You may be a king,' said the sage. 'But it is not for you to dictate where Kamadhenu should stay. She is quite content here in the ashram. I am sure she prefers the simple life and quiet atmosphere of this hermitage to the luxuries you might provide. With due apologies, I have to refuse your request.'

The king could not believe his ears! 'You dare to

refuse me!' he shouted. 'It seems you underestimate my might, O Vashishth. Do not forget I have an army with me. I asked you to give her to me politely. Now that you have refused my request, I will take her by force.'

Vashishth remained untroubled. All he said was, 'Take her if you can.'

Vishwamitra was too enraged to pay heed. He was already barking orders to the commander of his force.

'Seize the cow!' he cried.

The soldier advanced towards Kamadhenu. As he tried to grab her, she simply moved away. The commander tried again, but once again Kamadhenu evaded him.

'Hurry, help him!' bellowed the king. More soldiers dashed forward and surrounded the cow.

The ashram dwellers came running to see what the commotion was about. They stood there stunned at this violence that had suddenly disrupted the peace of the ashram.

'Guruji, do something to save our Kamadhenu!' they pleaded.

'Do not worry,' Vashishth said. 'She is quite safe. A smile flickered on his face.

More of the king's troops had encircled Kamadhenu now. But as they came closer, they were shocked to find that a horde of armed men had sprung up from the earth. They launched a fierce attack on the king's soldiers and pushed them back.

'Where did these come from? Drive them away!' shouted the king.

The rest of Vishwamitra's force leapt into the fray. A ferocious battle was fought. But in the end, the king's army was roundly defeated. They had to run for their lives.

'Stop, you cowards!' Vishwamitra cried, furious at this rout. 'Stand and fight!'

'We fought with all our might, your majesty,' replied the commander as he was fleeing. 'But there were too many of them. What's more, they were not real, human soldiers, but supernatural beings. Please, your majesty! You must also leave immediately. Your life is not safe here.'

The king cursed again, filled with helpless rage. Utterly humiliated, he was forced to ride away from the hermitage and seething with anger, he escaped. It was unbearable that he had to accept defeat at the hands of an ascetic. Of what use were all the trappings of a state when a man without any worldly belongings had proved to be stronger than him?

As he galloped back to the city, Vishwamitra was compelled to acknowledge a bitter truth—that real power did not lie with rulers of kingdoms. It lay with ascetics who had renounced everything.

He made a life-changing decision then. Instead of ruling as a monarch, he decided to devote himself to fasting and penance. He, too, would gain extraordinary powers by the strength of his will—powers that would make him superior to Vashishth. And one day, he vowed, he would avenge this disgrace.

Vishwamitra gave up his throne and all the pomp that accompanied it. Wearing the humble robes of an ascetic, he went deep into the forest. He began the most rigorous penance possible. Though he was a kshatriya, he was determined to be a man of learning, a sage like Vashishth. And he waited for the day when he would be able to get even with Vashishth.

How Indra Regained His Throne

Indra, the king of the gods, reigned in his heavenly capital Amravati. As an all-powerful god, he led an enviable life with his devoted wife Shachi. But the truth was, like other rulers, his position was not completely secure. He had many rivals who eyed his throne and constantly plotted to overthrow him.

One day, while they were seated on their thrones, Shachi had a sudden premonition that something unpropitious was about to happen. She told Indra about it, but he dismissed it as a figment of her imagination.

Little did he know that at that very moment a son had been born to his old enemy Tvashta. This child was most unusual—it had three heads. Tvashta was overjoyed. 'He will be powerful enough to dethrone Indra,' he exulted. He named the baby Trishiras.

Right from his childhood, Tvashta filled Trishiras's mind with the desire to dethrone Indra and the belief that he could do so. Consequently, as soon he was old enough, Trishiras began a severe penance that would empower him enough to displace Indra.

When Indra learnt about this, he was disturbed. He immediately called the apsaras, the beautiful celestial maidens who could charm any man. He sent them to distract Trishiras and interrupt his tapasya. But Trishiras turned out to be too strong-willed for them. He continued to meditate with greater intensity, and as his powers increased, Indra's position became more and more shaky.

Desperate to save his throne, Indra threw his thunderbolt at Trishiras and killed him. But this meant that he had committed the heinous sin of killing a Brahmin, so he had to perform a long penance to atone for it. Once it was over, he returned to Amravati.

Tvashta was filled with grief and enraged at his son's untimely death. He vowed to get back at Indra. He performed a sacrifice, creating an invincible asura called Vritra who could destroy Indra and avenge Trishiras.

Vritra was an enormous creature with extraordinary powers—so gigantic that he dwarfed Indra when he attacked the god. Indra fought with all his might to defend himself. In retaliation, Vritra simply laughed and caught him between his teeth with the greatest of ease. Indra would have been destroyed in no time at all; but

fortunately, one of the gods shot the *jrimbhaka astra,* an arrow which made the giant yawn at him, and Indra managed to escape.

Overcome with fear, the gods turned to Vishnu for help. He advised them to make peace with Vritra and wait for an opportunity to kill him. He also agreed to help Indra when the moment came.

So Indra tried to negotiate a truce with Vritra. The asura agreed to keep off his attack under certain conditions. He said that the god must not try to kill him by day or by night, or by any weapon that was wet or dry, made of wood or stone. Indra had no choice but to agree.

The king of the heavens knew that this was a temporary truce and Vritra would continue to be a threat. He racked his brains for a method to do away with Vritra without breaking his promise. One evening, while both of them were standing by the seashore, he got a brainwave. Gazing at the sea foam, it struck him that it was not a weapon ... it was neither wet nor dry, made of neither wood nor stone. The time was also right because it was neither day nor night. He immediately sent a thought message to Vishnu for help. Vishnu hurried there at once and crept into the foam. When Indra threw a handful of it at Vritra, Vishnu's presence turned the light and fluffy substance into a deadly weapon. So deadly that it dealt the asura a mortal blow.

Vritra was dead. However, Indra felt that he had

deceived Vritra and was overcome by guilt. Unable to face the world, he ran away and hid in shame. As soon as Indra disappeared, darkness descended on the earth. People, animals, the whole of creation milled around, confused and terrified, wondering what would happen next. Criminals freely committed crimes, knowing that they could get away with it. Total chaos reigned. As the world descended into anarchy, the gods grew anxious. Matters were slipping out of control, and if they did not act soon, the future of mankind would be at stake.

They knew that this state of chaos was caused by the lack of a ruler in heaven; they knew that they would have to appoint someone suitable immediately. But who would be the right man to replace Indra? After much thought, they chose a person they felt was fit—King Nahusha, the son of Ayu, a learned and pious man full of excellent qualities. The only problem was that he was a mortal. The gods then decided to bestow on him all the divine powers essential for the king of the heavens.

Once this was accomplished, Nahusha ascended Indra's throne and also inherited all his privileges. Nahusha came to live in Indra's celestial palace; rode upon Indra's elephant Airavat and became the owner of the wish-fulfilling Kalpatru tree. At first, Nahusha was over-awed by the grandeur of his new position. He was grateful to the gods for this extraordinary change in his fortunes. He was humble and treated them with great courtesy. However, it did not take long for power to go to his head. Now he began to order the gods and holy sages about as if they were his servants.

Soon the day came when his eye fell on Shachi. When he learned that she was Indra's wife, he demanded that she be made his queen as well. Shachi was horrified and rushed to Brihaspati, the guru of the gods, for help.

'Have no fear,' Brihaspati said. 'Indra will return soon. In the meantime you can take shelter in my house.'

When he heard that Shachi was trying to evade him, Nahusha became furious. He sent for the gods and said, 'You did not oppose Indra when he indulged in all kinds of unrighteous acts, like tricking Vritra before killing him and finishing off Trishiras while he was performing penance. If you do not bring Shachi to me, you will have to bear the consequences. Do not forget I'm your king now.'

The gods were alarmed. They themselves had armed Nahusha with divine powers and now he was powerful enough to threaten them! However, they had little choice, so they rushed off to to fetch Shachi.

Shachi wept bitterly at the thought of being compelled to marry Nahusha. However, Brihaspati advised her to ask Nahusha to give her some time while he devised a plan to save her.

Shachi went to Nahusha and said, 'As you well know, I am a married woman. It would be a sin for both of us if I married you while my husband was alive. Let me try to trace him. If we cannot locate him, I promise to be your queen.'

Nahusha agreed. Once again the gods went and asked Vishnu for help. 'It was your power that actually caused Vritra's death,' they said, 'but Indra is hiding in shame because he feels he has committed a sin.'

Vishnu said, 'Find Indra and tell him to worship me and perform the horse sacrifice, the ashwamedha yagna, to atone for his crime and I will help him.'

After a long search the gods finally located Indra. They told him all that had happened since he disappeared, and begged him to come and claim his rightful place in heaven again. Indra then performed the sacrifice and came to Amravati to fight Nahusha. But when the moment to face him arrived, Indra was overcome with fear. His whole frame trembled and his knees knocked together. He turned around and ran away without fighting Nahusha.

Grief-stricken and desperate now, that night Shachi prayed fervently to Upashruti, the goddess of chastity, for help. Touched by her appeal, the goddess appeared and asked Shachi what she desired. 'Please take me to my husband,' Shachi pleaded.

It was a long and difficult journey because Indra was hiding in Lake Mansarovar. Upashruti led Shachi over high mountains till they arrived at a lake full of lotuses.

'He is hidden inside that big lotus,' Upashruti said. 'We will have to go underwater and slit the stem.'

Indra had reduced himself to the size of an atom and was hiding inside the lotus stem. Shachi dived into the lake along with Upashruti who then shrank Shachi as well.

'Now you can get inside the stem and speak to your husband,' she said.

Shachi squeezed into the lotus stem and came face to face with Indra. 'Why do you continue to hide here?' she asked. 'You are the king of heaven! You have to reclaim your throne! If not for anything else, you have to come back and help me. The evil Nahusha wants to make me his wife. I simply cannot bear the thought but no one can do anything about it! Even the gods are helpless because when they put him on your throne, they gave him many powers.'

Her appeal touched Indra and he came up with a plan to regain his throne and save Shachi.

Full of hope, Shachi returned to Amravati. The next morning, she told Nahusha, 'I have decided. Since Indra has run away, I will become your queen, but on one condition. He used to visit me in my palace mounted in various ways—sometimes on a horse, sometimes on his elephant and sometimes on his chariot. I want you to come on a palanquin carried by the seven sages.'

'That is no problem,' Nahusha said. He was so puffed up with pride that he did not think twice about ordering the highly respected Saptarishis to bear his palanquin on their shoulders.

Shachi then went and informed Brihaspati what she had

done. At once he performed a sacrifice and asked Agni, the god of fire, to find Indra and bring him back to Amravati.

In the meantime, Nahusha attired himself in rich garments and mounted the palanquin. He was so impatient to meet Shachi that he felt the sages were not moving as fast as he wanted. He noticed that Agastya was shorter than the others and decided that it was his fault. He prodded him with his foot, saying, 'Sarpa, sarpa,' the way one goads an elephant. Agastya was enraged at this insult. He turned around and cursed Nahusha, saying, '*Sarpo bhava*! May you turn into a snake!'

The conceited Nahusha was instantly transformed into a snake and fell writhing from the heavens to the earth. It would take him several hundred years to regain his human form.

In the meantime, Agni and the other gods had located Indra and prevailed on him to return. As they reached Amravati, Agastya greeted them with the news that Nahusha had been changed into a snake and Indra could once again occupy his throne.

Indra and Shachi were reunited and all was well in Amravati once more, thanks to the efforts of the faithful and devoted Shachi.

Faithful Jatayu

After being banished from Ayodhya for fourteen years, Ram headed for the forest along with his devoted wife Sita and faithful brother Lakshman. Following the sage Bharadwaj's advice, they travelled to Panchavati. While they were on their way, they were startled at the sight of an enormous vulture.

'Who are you?' they asked, believing him to be a rakshasa.

To their surprise, the vulture replied in a gentle and sweet voice, 'I am Jatayu, Aruna's son, a friend of your father's. I am a descendent of the creators of the world, the Prajapatis.'

Ram was overjoyed to discover a friend of his father's in the deep forest. He bowed low to Jatayu and embraced him.

'If you wish, dear child,' Jatayu said, 'I can stay with

you. The forest is full of dangers. I can protect Sita when you and Lakshman happen to be away."

Ram accepted his offer gladly and Jatayu accompanied them to Panchavati. When they reached, they were delighted to find that Panchavati was a beautiful forest, full of flowering trees. As they searched for a site to build their hermitage, Ram came across a charming spot close to a lake. The lake was full of multi-coloured lotuses, including the rare blue ones. Swans and other water birds flocked on the lake and herds of deer pranced on its banks. The river Godavari flowed near it too, and closeby were gentle rolling hills that looked like huge elephants.

The brothers and Sita settled down happily in this enchanting place along with Jatayu, and all was going well.

Then one day, as they were sitting in their thatched hut, a strange woman passed by. She stopped to greet them, and told them that her name was Shurpnakha and that she was the sister of Ravan, the ten-headed king of Lanka, which meant she was a rakshasi.

Shurpnakha smiled enticingly at Ram. 'It is very fortunate that I found you here in the forest,' she said. 'My own husband is no more and I would like to marry again. I think you would be the perfect mate for me.'

At first Ram was taken aback. Then he quickly said, 'I am sorry, but I have to turn down your proposal. I happen to be a married man and am devoted to my wife Sita. She is here with me.' He threw a mischievous smile at Lakshman and continued, 'Maybe you can try asking my younger brother.'

Shurpnakha turned to Lakshman and said, 'You are a little young for me but what do years matter? I am still a fine figure of a woman. Many admire my beautiful eyes.'

'You are not exactly what I want in a wife,' Lakshman replied. 'I think my brother Ram would suit you better.'

Lakshman meant it as a joke. But Shurpnakha cried, 'Then I will have to get rid of his wife!'

She swung around and raised her hand to attack Sita. Horrified, Lakshman immediately pulled out his sword to defend his sister-in-law. In his rage, he lopped off Shurpnakha's ears and nose.

The rakshasi let out a horrible shriek. 'What have you done, you wretched man? You have disfigured me! You will pay a heavy price for this when my brothers come to avenge me.'

The whole forest rang with Shurpnakha's screams as she ran to tell her brother Khar, who lived not too far away, what had happened. Furious, he sent seven of his men to kill Ram and Lakshman.

But Ram and Lakshman were more than a match for the rakshasas. They finished them off in no time. Maddened with rage, Shurpnakha went back to Khar urging him to destroy the two brothers who had insulted her.

This time Khar took his brother Dushan and fourteen thousand rakshasas along. But Ram and Lakshman wiped out their army and killed both Khar and Dushan as well.

However, one of the rakshasas, Akampana, managed to escape. He rushed to Lanka to inform Khar and Dushan's brother Ravan about the deaths. Ravan, who believed he was invincible, was outraged to hear that Ram and Lakshman had vanquished a whole army of rakshasas by themselves.

'How could just the two of them decimate this large force?' he bellowed. 'And finish off my brothers too? I will teach them a lesson they will not forget!'

'Wait, mighty king. There is another way to take revenge,' the cunning Akampana said. 'Ram might be invincible in battle, but it does not mean that he is not vulnerable. Listen to me. His wife Sita is beautiful beyond compare. She would add greatly to the lustre of your harem. Ram is deeply devoted to her. If you carry her off, he will be overcome with grief and you will find it easy to slay him.'

Ravan thought this over for a while. Then he set out on his Pushpak Vimana, the flying chariot that could carry him to distant places in no time. He decided to consult his uncle Marich first, a rakshasa who had repented for his evil ways and was living as a hermit on the coast. When he heard his plans, Marich said, 'You have been given wrong advice, dear nephew. I have had two encounters with Ram and both times I had to flee to save my life. It would be wisest to return to Lanka and leave Ram and

Sita alone, otherwise you risk the destruction of our race.'

Ravan was convinced and went back to Lanka.

However, soon after he returned, Shurpnakha arrived at his palace, howling with rage. 'See what Ram and Lakshman have done to me!' she screamed. 'And you sit here without a care in the world. A ruler who does not take action against his enemies will without doubt be destroyed by them.'

The sight of his mutilated sister acted as a red flag to Ravan. 'Wipe your tears, Shurpnakha, I swear to avenge you!' he thundered. 'Ram and Lakshman will learn what it means to attack a member of my family.'

Ravan rushed to Marich again to ask for his support. Once more Marich tried to persuade him not to abduct Sita. But Ravan threatened to kill him if he did not help. Marich had no choice. Reluctantly, he climbed into Ravan's chariot and the two reached Ram's ashram.

Sita was gathering flowers at the time, quite unaware of the danger lurking nearby. Together, Ravan and Marich hatched a scheme to trick her. Marich used his magic powers to transform himself into a beautiful golden deer studded with all kinds of jewels. He gambolled about in front of Sita to attract her. Sita was enchanted at the sight.

'Please, can you catch that beautiful deer for me?' she asked Ram. 'I would love to keep it as a pet.'

'It's not a real deer,' Lakshman said, casting a suspicious look at the deer. 'It's an illusion created by Marich. It is best to leave it alone.'

'I'm sure it is—it looks very real,' Sita insisted.

'It looks real to me, too,' Ram said, gazing at the animal. 'A captivating creature indeed. If you fear it is an illusion created to lead us into danger, Lakshman, for safety's sake why don't you stay here with Sita along with Jatayu? If it is Marich, I will kill it and thus put an end to that evil sorcerer.'

Ram ran after the deer that was prancing among the trees. The deer led Ram on a merry chase. Finally Ram let loose an arrow that pierced the animal fatally. As he was breathing his last, Marich shrieked out in Ram's voice, 'Hai Sita! Hai Lakshman!'

Sita started up as she heard his cry. Panic-stricken, terrified that something had happened to Ram, she cried, 'Go and help him, Lakshman! I fear the worst!'

'But my brother told me to stay here and take care of you,' Lakshman protested. 'How can I flout his wishes?'

'If you don't go, it means you don't care for your brother!' Sita wept, beside herself with anxiety.

Lakshman was in a quandary. Finally he rose and took up his bow and arrows. 'I will go since you insist, although it's against my better judgement,' he said. 'But I am drawing a protective circle around the hut to keep you safe. On no condition must you step outside it.' After drawing the circle, Lakshman reluctantly left.

No sooner did he go out of sight than Ravan appeared

in the form of a wandering sadhu asking for alms. Conscious of the hospitality due to a guest, Sita offered him food and water. However, she took care to stay within the line Lakshman had drawn.

'Unless you step out of that circle, I cannot accept anything from you, kind lady,' Ravan said cunningly.

Sita hesitated. But she was uneasy about flouting the laws of hospitality and displeasing a holy man, so she stepped forward with the food and water.

The moment she put a foot across the line of protection, Ravan returned to his real form and grabbed her. His golden flying chariot appeared immediately and he dragged the screaming Sita into it.

Jatayu, who was perched on a nearby tree, was startled at the sight. 'Jatayu, O dear Jatayu!' Sita cried, 'I beg you to call Ram and Lakshman! Tell them that Ravan is carrying me away!'

Jatayu tried to reason with Ravan. 'O proud king of the rakshasas, listen to me,' he said. 'I am Jatayu, the king of the vultures. I have studied the Puranas and know what dharma is. Do not commit such an evil act. Leave Sita alone. She is another man's wife. And if you don't listen to me, I will do my utmost to prevent you from taking her away. I am sixty thousand years old, you are young and well-armed, but do not think I cannot battle with you!'

This infuriated Ravan. 'You will teach me dharma? You will stop me?' he snarled. 'I'll give you a taste of what

I can do.' He turned and swung his sword at Jatayu.

Jatayu fought back bravely. First, he killed the rakshasa-headed mules that drew Ravan's chariot. He tore at the chariot with his claws and damaged the canopy with his great wings.

Ravan slashed at Jatayu with his right hand, holding on to Sita with his left. In turn, Jatayu cut off Ravan's ten left arms with his beak. But they grew back immediately. Ravan let Sita go and attacked Jatayu with all his might. He lopped off his wings and his claws. Despite his efforts to fight back, the giant vulture was mortally wounded and fell to earth, dying. Sita ran to his side, weeping bitterly. She tried to embrace the faithful bird, but Ravan dragged her away. As the chariot flew off, the flowers from Sita's hair fell like rain on Jatayu's body.

In the meantime, Ram saw Lakshman running towards him, and got worried.

'Why have you come here?' he cried. Lakshman explained what had happened.

'You should not have left Sita alone, no matter what she said,' Ram said. 'Let us go back at once. I fear the worst.'

They rushed back to the ashram and were horrified to find Sita missing. Almost mad with anxiety, they searched high and low along the banks of the Godavari, then scoured the forest nearby.

And then they came across their friend Jatayu lying in a pool of blood.

Jatayu just about had the strength to whisper, 'Ravan, the rakshasa king, has abducted Sita. He cut off my wings and has taken her south. I am dying, Ram, but do not despair. You will win Sita back after killing Ravan.'

'Tell me more, noble bird!' Ram cried out. But Jatayu's eyes were closing. His breath became fainter and fainter and finally stopped.

Heartbroken, Ram lit a funeral pyre and cremated Jatayu with all the honour due to a close relative. Then, along with Lakshman, he headed south in search of Sita.

The Tale of a Ring

Indra, the king of the gods, was deeply troubled. The sage Vishwamitra had embarked on a rigorous course of self-denial. He sat without moving, in the lotus position, deep in meditation. He had not eaten or even drunk water for a very long time. His enormous powers of concentration helped him to control his bodily functions and thus remain alive.

Indra well knew what would happen when a holy man embarked on such a course. He would gain much merit. And if he kept it up long enough, he could become more powerful than the king of gods.

No wonder the mighty Indra was worried!

I have to do something, he thought desperately. Vishwamitra must be made to abandon his penance. But how?

Then an idea came to him in a flash.

Indra summoned Menaka. She was one of the most beautiful of the apsaras, the celestial dancers at his court. 'Menaka,' he said, 'I need your help. You must go and end Vishwamitra's penance.'

'I cannot refuse you, my lord,' Menaka replied. 'But you know Vishwamitra not only has extraordinary powers but also a terrible temper. What if he gets annoyed and reduces me to a pinch of ash?'

'You are right,' Indra said. 'He is a dangerous man.'

Menaka said, 'If you send Kama, the god of love, and Marut, the god of wind, to help me, we may be able to accomplish this together.'

'That's an excellent idea,' Indra said. He immediately ordered Kama and Marut to accompany the apsara.

The two gods flew with Menaka to the barren mountaintop where Vishwamitra was meditating. Using their powers, the gods turned it into a garden blooming with beautiful flowers that filled the air with the sweetest of fragrances. But Vishwamitra continued to sit unaffected, with his eyes closed. Then the wind god blew a scented breeze straight into his face. So intoxicating was its fragrance that it distracted the holy man. He opened his eyes with a start. The first person he saw was Menaka standing before him. At that very moment, the god of love shot an arrow into his heart.

Vishwamitra was deeply smitten. He abandoned his penance right away.

Vishwamitra and Menaka spent a few years together. After some time she gave birth to a pretty baby girl. But by this time Menaka was beginning to miss the excitement and luxuries of Indra's court. So, one day, she left Vishwamitra and the baby in a valley near the river Malini and flew back to heaven. Vishwamitra was heartbroken. Distracted with grief, he too abandoned the baby and wandered into the forest.

As the helpless baby lay alone, some kind-hearted birds saw her and were saddened by her plight. They took care of her needs and protected her from wild animals.

One day, another holy man, the Rishi Kanva, came to bathe in the river. He was surprised to find a baby on the bank, surrounded by birds. He picked her up and took her to his ashram. Because 'shakuns', or birds, had looked after her, he named her 'Shakuntala'.

Shakuntala lived in the hermitage as the rishi's daughter. There she grew into a beautiful young woman. One day, the king of the country, Dushyant, came to hunt in the forest. He decided to pay his respects to the rishi, who was known for his wisdom and piety. However, Rishi Kanva had gone into the forest to gather fruit and herbs, and only Shakuntala was at the ashram. She offered the king fruit and water and asked him to wait for the sage to return.

The king was intrigued to find such a charming girl at the ashram. 'Who are you?' he asked. 'I know Rishi Kanva is unmarried, so you cannot be his daughter.'

Shakuntala told him the story of her birth. The king found it fascinating. He said, 'You are the loveliest girl I have ever met. And after hearing the story of your birth, I feel you are a suitable bride for me. Will you marry me, Shakuntala?'

Shakuntala was astounded at this unexpected proposal. But she, too, was attracted to the handsome young king. And she had heard her father speak highly of Dushyant. However, she said, 'I am deeply honoured by your proposal, but I must ask for my father's permission before I agree.'

The king replied, 'The rishi has brought you up well. But you are old enough to make your own decisions. You should be able to choose your husband yourself.'

Shakuntala thought this over. Then she said, 'I will marry you on one condition—you must promise that my son will rule the country after you.'

The king said, 'As God is my witness, the son born from you will be my successor.'

The couple then exchanged garlands of flowers, which was an accepted form of marriage at that time. The king took off his signet ring and put it on Shakuntala's finger. 'This is proof that I have taken you as my wife,' he said.

The sun had already sunk behind the trees now, and it was getting dark. But the sage had not yet returned.

Finally Dushyant said, 'It is getting very late. My retainers are waiting for me on the outskirts of the forest. They must be getting anxious. We should leave now.'

'But I cannot leave without informing my father,' Shakuntala replied.

'You're right,' said the king. 'The sage will be worried if he finds you gone. But I cannot stay any longer. I have to go. I'll send my soldiers and priests for you when I get back. They will escort you to my palace.'

Dushyant left.

When Rishi Kanva returned, Shakuntala told him everything. 'You did the right thing,' he said. 'Dushyant is good and noble, a man most fit to be your husband.'

A few days later, Shakuntala was sitting outside the hermitage, lost in thought, when a visitor arrived. It was the Rishi Durvasa, a man known for his quick temper. Shakuntala was so preoccupied that she did not notice the holy man and failed to greet him. Only when the sage cleared his throat did she spring up to bow before him. But the damage had already been done. The rishi felt extremely insulted.

'Is this how you treat your elders?' he thundered. And in the heat of his anger, he laid a terrible curse on Shakuntala. 'May the person you were thinking of when you ignored me lose all memory of you!' he said.

Shakuntala was stunned. Such a severe punishment for such a small mistake! She fell at the rishi's feet, weeping. 'Please, holy sir,' she begged, 'take back your curse. I am willing to perform any penance as punishment for my ill-manneredness.' Shakuntala had good reason to be disturbed. She had been thinking of Dushyant when the rishi came to the ashram.

When he saw what a devastating affect his curse had had on the young woman, the rishi's anger evaporated. He said in a gentler tone, 'My daughter, a curse can never be taken back. However, all I can say is that if you show him anything he has given you, his memory will return.'

Shakuntala cheered up at once. She had the ring Dushyant had given her. It would serve as an antidote to the curse.

Days turned into months, and the king who had forgotten his bride did not send for Shakuntala. By now she had discovered that she was with child. Her father suggested that they go to the court and remind Dushyant that he had married her. 'My daughter,' said the rishi, 'do not deprive your child of a father. Go to the king. When he sees the ring, he will remember you.'

Shakuntala prepared for the journey to Dushyant's palace. The thought of being reunited with Dushyant filled her with joy, but it was hard to part from her loving father and the inhabitants of the ashram who were like brothers and sisters to her.

Rishi Kanva sent some of his disciples to accompany her, saying, 'A girl should not go to her husband's home alone.'

On the way they had to cross a river. While she was sitting in the boat, Shakuntala could not resist trailing her hand in the cool water. Lost in thought, she didn't notice when her ring fell off. A fish swimming below the boat darted up and swallowed it at once.

The simple ashram dwellers were overcome with awe by the sights they saw in Dushyant's magnificent capital city. And when they reached his palace, they were even more wonder-struck by its grandeur. But when they got to the door, the guards wouldn't let them in.

Shakuntala held her ground, saying that she would not leave without seeing the king. The sound of their argument reached Dushyant, who sent for them.

'Who are you, woman?' he asked. 'And what do you want from me?'

Shakuntala's eyes filled with tears. 'So you really have forgotten me,' she said. 'After making all those promises.'

'What promises are you talking about?' asked the king, confused.

'You married me in the forest and promised to send for me,' Shakuntala said. 'This is the ring you put on my finger ...' She looked down at her finger. But the ring was no longer there! 'You ... you did give me a ring,' she stammered. 'I ... I seem to have lost it.'

Dushyant was furious. 'Woman,' he said, 'be thankful that I am taking pity on your condition and not punishing you for your terrible lies. Leave the court right away!'

Full of despair, the little group returned to Rishi Kanva's ashram.

'Do not give up hope, my daughter,' said the sage, consoling the weeping Shakuntala. 'The day will surely come when the king will acknowledge you and your child.'

Time passed and Shakuntala gave birth to a boy. She named him Bharat and brought him up with much love. The rishi taught him his letters and trained him in the martial arts.

Bharat turned out to be an extraordinarily brave child. He played with all the wild animals in the forest and thought nothing of wrestling with tigers and lions.

One day a fisherman caught an enormous fish. He felt it was fit only for the king's table, so he took it to the royal kitchen and sold it to the head cook. When the cook cut the fish open, he found a beautiful ring. And when he examined it closely he realised it was the king's signet ring. He took it to Dushyant right away. The moment the king laid eyes on the ring, his memories of Shakuntala returned.

'I am guilty of a great injustice,' he cried. 'I refused to recognise the woman I love. I must go and ask her forgiveness right away.'

Dushyant made preparations to leave for the forest

immediately and set off in a grand procession, with the royal priests and retainers dressed in colourful uniforms, bearing many gifts of silken clothes and precious jewels for his wife and child.

When the king reached the hermitage, an amazing sight greeted him—that of a sturdy little boy playing with a tiger. The little boy had opened the tiger's mouth and was counting his teeth.

'Aren't you afraid, my child?' Dushyant asked, wonderstruck.

The child looked up at him. 'No,' he said. 'Why should I be afraid?'

'Whose son are you?' Dushyant asked, full of wonder at the boy's strength and daring.

'I am Bharat, the son of Shakuntala,' said the boy. 'Who are you?'

'I am King Dushyant,' said the king. 'Where is your mother?'

Hearing the sound of voices, Shakuntala came out of the ashram. But when she set eyes on the king, she stopped short. Memories of the humiliation she had suffered at his court came flooding back.

'Shakuntala ... I know I did not treat you right when you came to my palace. For some reason, I could not recognise you at that time. I had no recollection of you at all. Can you ever forgive me?' Dushyant asked before she could speak.

'It was not your fault,' Shakuntala said with a sad smile. She told him about Rishi Durvasa's curse.

'To think that you had to pay so heavily for that small mistake! But there is something I must know immediately. Is this extraordinary child my son?' Dushyant asked eagerly.

'Yes, this is your son, Bharat,' Shakuntala replied.

'He already possesses the qualities of a great ruler,' Dushyant said, gazing lovingly at the boy. 'You have brought him up well.'

Just then Rishi Kanva arrived on the scene. Dushyant fell at his feet and begged forgiveness for the great wrong he had done to his daughter.

In return, the kind rishi gave him his blessings.

Dushyant took Shakuntala and Bharat back to his palace with much pomp and show. He crowned her queen and announced Bharat as his heir.

Bharat was a great ruler and the forefather of a line of powerful kings. His country, India, was named Bharatvarsha after him.

When Vishnu Became a Fish

Brahma, the creator, was exhausted. He had been busy creating the universe and now his day, equal to a kalpa or 4.32 billion years in human time, was over. As he got ready to sleep, he yawned. But as he opened his mouth in an enormous yawn, the Vedas slipped out of it. Two demons named Madhu and Kaitabha had been lying in wait for just this opportunity. They wanted to steal these important scriptures for their people, the danavs, who were always at war with the gods. They made off with the Vedas and hid them in the ocean.

In the meantime, a king called Manu was performing a rigorous penance. Being the child of Vivaswat the Sun, he was known as Vaivasvata Manu and was a very pious man. He was not interested in wielding power as a king or enjoying the pomp of office. Consequently, he had given up his throne to his son and decided to devote his life to prayer and fasting. He chose a quiet spot in his kingdom in the Malabar region of Kerala. Deep inside the lush green forests, he began to perform a tapasya which had already lasted for a million years.

The tapasya meant that Manu did not eat any food and survived only on water. One day, as he scooped up a handful of water from the river Kritimala to offer an oblation to the gods, a small fish swam into his cupped palms. To his surprise, it began to speak. 'Please help me, holy sir,' it said. 'I am so small that I'm afraid to live in this big river. The larger fish will gobble me up in no time. I will be very grateful if you put me in a container where I will be safe. And I would really appreciate it if you would be kind enough to take care of me.'

Manu realised at once that this was no ordinary fish and felt he was being entrusted with an important responsibility. In any case, he was compassionate towards all living creatures. So he put the fish into a beautiful jar that was as bright as a moon beam. He looked after it well, feeding it at the right times and changing the water in the jar whenever necessary. After some time he noticed that the little fish was growing. When it doubled its proportions, he was more than a little surprised. And as time passed, the fish grew at such speed that it soon filled the jar and there was no place left for it to move about.

'Noble king, I need more space now,' it said to Manu one day. 'This jar has become too cramped for me.'

'That's what I noticed too. I think you are large enough to be put in a pond now,' Manu said.

'Please do it quickly,' said the fish.

Manu searched in the forest and found a good, clean pond where there were no other fish to threaten it, and placed his fish there.

But the fish continued to grow. Each day it added to its length and girth. And sure enough, the time came when it was too big for the pond.

Again it spoke, saying, 'I have outgrown this pond now, dear king. Please put me into a river where I will have enough space to swim around.'

Manu carried the fish to the river Ganga and slipped it into the water. He was convinced now that this was no ordinary fish. But he knew that the fish would reveal who it was at the appropriate time and decided to wait patiently for that moment.

The fish went on increasing in size. And to Manu's amazement, the day came when even the mighty Ganga was too small for it.

'Good king, this river is a tight squeeze. The ocean is the only place vast enough for me now,' the fish told him. 'Please take me there.'

Manu hauled the supernatural fish to the ocean and pushed it in. But before it swam away, it spoke again. 'I am very grateful to you for taking such good care of me, O king,' it said. 'Now I am large enough to survive the worst of calamities and there is a reason behind this. Please listen to me carefully. I have something important to tell you.'

Manu was very curious to know who the fish was and what it wanted to share. By now he had guessed that all that had happened earlier was preparation for something significant. 'Speak, noble being,' he said. 'I am all attention.'

'I'm sorry to inform you that the world has become too evil,' the fish said. 'It needs to be purified. However, the only way to do this is to destroy it totally and start afresh. In seven days, a mighty flood, the *pralaya,* is going to descend on the earth and drown everything. Because you are pure of heart and have performed so many good deeds, you have been chosen as the human being who will be saved to start life afresh once the flood has receded.'

Manu was stunned. Total destruction of the earth! What a terrible thing. But he knew he could not change what had been decreed, so he prostrated himself on the ground and asked, 'Great being, please reveal yourself. And kindly advise me how I should save myself.'

The moment he said this, Vishnu appeared in all his divine glory. Manu was dazzled by the sight, but somehow managed to keep his wits about him.

'You must build a mighty ship,' Vishnu said. 'You will need to attach a long rope to it. This rope must be very strong and none other than Vasuki, the great serpent, will be equal to the task of pulling this ship. Then go and consult the seven great sages, Vashishth, Bharadwaj, Jamadagni, Gautam, Atri, Vishwamitra and Agastya. They will guide you in gathering together all the seeds of life—herbs and animals that will be essential to restock the new world. When the deluge begins, go on board carrying these seeds, along with the Saptarishis. When the entire earth is completely covered with water, call out to me. I will arrive in the form of a matsya, and you will be able to recognise me by my horn. I will save you.'

With these words, Vishnu in his matsyavatar plunged into the ocean and vanished from sight.

Manu turned back, deeply preoccupied. He was full of grief at the thought that all life would be wiped out on earth. But he was well aware of how evil had spread its tentacles throughout the world. This, perhaps, was the only way to root it out and for life to start afresh.

Manu did what the matsyavatar had advised. He began to build the ship and requested Vasuki to act as the rope. When it was complete, he went to the seven holy sages and asked for their help. The sages instructed him how to gather the seeds of life to put on the boat.

Manu had barely finished all these tasks when dark clouds gathered across the sky and it began to rain heavily. It poured and poured day after day, night after night, week after week. The rivers began to overflow and water flooded the fields and started to enter the cities. People fled for their lives and tried to reach the highest places where they would be safe.

But the downpour did not let up. The waters rose higher and higher and soon there was hardly a place that was not under water. Everyone and everything drowned and all life perished on earth. Manu and the seven rishis were the only ones who survived. They were safe on the ship that floated safely on the water.

Manu kept a lookout for the fish and at last he sighted it, recognising it by its horn. He bowed low to it and then took the rope, which was the serpent Vasuki, and tied it to the fish's horn.

The huge fish pulled the ship through the flood waters, and along the way, it spoke to Manu and passed on the highest forms of knowledge to him. It revealed the Vedas, the Samhitas and the Puranas to Manu, as well as the Supreme Truth.

At last they reached the only piece of land that remained uncovered—the highest peak of the Himalayas.

'Tie the rope firmly to the peak,' the fish said, coming to a stop.

Manu and the seven rishis did so. (This event is known as the 'naubandhana' or the binding of the ship and the word also means harbour.)

'When the waters begin to recede, you must descend right away,' the fish warned them. 'Otherwise you will remain stuck here forever.'

Lord Vishnu then revealed himself to Manu and said, 'I assumed this form to preserve life on earth. Now create life afresh as soon as the flood waters have drained away completely. This is the duty allotted to you.'

Manu bowed low. 'I am greatly honoured,' he said. 'And I thank you for choosing me for this task. I will perform it to the best of my ability.'

But matsyavatar had something more to do. He had to capture Madhu and Kaitabha and recover the Vedas. He killed the danavs and returned the Vedas to Brahma, who was just waking up after the end of a long night.

Manu followed Vishnu's instructions and peopled a new world with the seeds of life that he had carried with him on the ship. Thus he became the forefather of mankind reborn.

The Baby Who Talked Too Much

Uddalak was a sage famous for his learning and many students thronged his ashram to acquire knowledge of the Vedas. Among them was a young man named Kahola.

Kahola turned out to be an excellent student. So good was he that Uddalak felt he had a bright future and decided to get his daughter Sujata married to him.

Soon Sujata became pregnant and all her thoughts began to revolve around the welfare of the child she was carrying. It was believed that if a baby in the womb was exposed to spiritual discourses and the chanting of the scriptures, it would absorb all that knowledge. As the daughter and wife of two great scholars, Sujata wanted her unborn child to benefit from their learning. She was confident that if she attended their classes regularly, her baby would turn out to be a genius and surpass all the erudite men of his age. So, Sujata joined the students as they listened to Uddalak and Kahola chanting Vedic mantras and instructing them in other fields of knowledge.

Sujata listened to whatever was being taught with all her attention. And soon it became obvious that her dedication was benefiting the unborn child enormously, though in a somewhat unexpected way.

One day, as Kahola was reciting the Vedas for the benefit of his students, he enunciated one syllable incorrectly. After listening to the Vedas being recited regularly, the baby was now well-versed in the correct pronunciation of each and every syllable of each verse of the Vedas. When it heard his father speak incorrectly, it writhed within Sujata's womb as if it was in pain. And much to everyone's astonishment, a voice emerged from her belly, 'Pitashree, you are not reciting this verse correctly.'

Both teacher and students turned around to gaze at Sujata. Kahola's face went red with anger. He was enraged that his own offspring was pointing out his mistakes and humiliating him in front of his students! He was aghast that a baby not yet fully formed, who had not even entered the world, claimed to be more knowledgeable than him!

'How dare you challenge me, your own father, you impudent infant?' he cried. 'Since my chanting has irked you so much, the part of your body that you moved will become crooked. You will be born deformed.'

Sujata was horrified but she hoped this curse would not really have any effect on the foetus. A few days later Kahola mispronounced a syllable once again while rendering a verse. Once again the baby squirmed in his mother's womb. And once again a voice emerged from Sujata's belly, saying, 'Pitashree, wrong again!'

Kahola was furious. This half-formed fledgling was so brash that even his father's rebuke did not deter him from speaking out! He cursed the baby a second time saying that the part he had moved now would also be disfigured. However, Kahola's admonitions did not deter the foetus and he continued to challenge his father whenever Kahola made a mistake. Thus, he questioned Kahola eight times in all, and each time the sage cursed him.

Sujata now knew that the child growing in her womb was going to be an extraordinary scholar. If he had acquired mastery over the Vedas even before he was born, what feats would he be capable of when he was fully grown? She didn't worry too much about her husband's curses. She was more concerned about her child's future and wanted Kahola to earn enough money so her child would receive the best upbringing possible.

She soon heard that King Janak was organising a great yagya, or fire sacrifice. Believing this to be a wonderful opportunity, she asked Kahola to go and participate in the ceremony. The king would definitely reward all the attending Brahmins handsomely.

Kahola also thought this was a good idea and set off on his journey. But when he arrived at Janak's palace, he was taken aback to find that the king's plans had changed. Janak received him respectfully as a man of learning, but told him, 'It is true, noble teacher, that I had planned this sacrifice for many years. But even as my preparations were under way, the great sage Bandin suddenly arrived. He insisted that I begin the sacrifice only after he was defeated in a shashtrartha or a debate on the scriptures, by another learned man. He laid down the condition that he would immerse those whom he vanquished under water. Not wishing to offend him, I agreed.'

'Immerse them under water? What kind of condition is that?' Kahola asked.

The king's face turned grim. 'I am afraid Bandin has already defeated many learned scholars. He drowned them in the river.'

'What?' Kahola was shocked. Then he said, after thinking for a moment, 'I will be very happy to participate in a discussion with Bandin. It would give me great satisfaction to defeat this arrogant man and avenge the death of all those unfortunate men.'

Kahola was quite confident about his ability to hold his own in any debate on the scriptures. Unfortunately, he turned out to be no match for the wily Bandin. According to the defined condition, Bandin immersed Kahola in a nearby river.

When Sujata received the news, she was disconsolate. 'It is entirely my fault!' she wailed. 'Oh, how I wish I hadn't sent him to King Janak's court! What will happen to my poor baby now? This brilliant child will grow up without a father.' She wept bitterly.

Her father, Uddalak, tried to console her as best he could. 'Kahola cannot come back,' he said, wiping his tears. 'But do not be anxious about your baby's future. I will be like a father to him. You will not have to worry about anything.'

Soon after, Sujata gave birth to a boy. But when she set eyes on the baby, she cried out in horror. Kahola's curse had been effective, after all. The infant's body was deformed in eight places—his two feet, knees, hands, chest and head were askew. Consequently, he was named Ashtavakra, which means 'one with eight bends.'

Uddalak summoned all the inhabitants of the hermitage and made an announcement. 'As I said earlier, I will bring up this child as my own son. And I swear you all to secrecy. No one must disclose to Ashtavakra when he is old enough to understand that his real father is dead.'

By a strange coincidence, almost at the same time, a son was born to Uddalak too. This boy was named Shvetaketu. The two boys were raised together. Thus

Ashtavakra grew up believing that Uddalak was his father and Shvetaketu his brother.

Uddalak educated both of them at his ashram. Fulfilling the promise he had displayed even in the womb, Ashtavakra proved to possess extraordinary intelligence. By the age of twelve he had acquired knowledge beyond what most scholars attained in a lifetime.

But in some ways he remained a child. He was deeply attached to Uddalak who displayed as much love for Ashtavakra as he did for his own son Shvetaketu. One day, Ashtavakra affectionately climbed onto Uddalak's lap. Just then Shvetaketu arrived on the scene and overcome with jealousy, pulled him off.

'Why are you doing this? What's the matter?' Ashtavakra asked, shocked.

'You have no right to sit on my father's lap. You are not his son! I am!' Shvetaketu said angrily.

'Is that true, Pitashree?' Ashtavakra cried out. 'Who is my father then?'

Uddalak turned pale. 'What have you done, you thoughtless boy?' he said to Shvetaketu. 'My dear child,' he told Ashtavakra gently, 'please ask your mother what happened to your father.'

Ashtavakra ran to his mother. 'Is it true?' he asked Sujata. 'That I am not the great sage Uddalak's son? Ma, tell me at once if this is so. Why was this kept from me?'

His mother put her arms around him. 'I should

have realised that you would find out one day,' she said, brushing away a tear. 'My son, the great sage Uddalak is your grandfather. Your father was a learned scholar and was his disciple. Unfortunately, he was defeated in a shastrartha by a cruel man named Bandin at King Janak's court just before you were born. Bandin had laid a condition in the competition that he would drown all those he vanquished. Unfortunately, your father was defeated and thus met the same fate as many other learned Brahmins.'

'You should have told me earlier, Ma!' Ashtavakra cried out. 'I will challenge this evil man and avenge my father's death.'

'My boy, you are too young!' Sujata wept. 'I will not be able to bear it if you too become a victim of Bandin's wiles.'

'No, mother, my mind is made up!' Ashtavakra said determinedly.

When mother and son went to Uddalak, the sage said, 'Let the boy go, Sujata. He possesses extraordinary intelligence. Maybe he is destined to put an end to Bandin's course of destruction.'

Then a chastised Shvetaketu said hesitantly, 'Will you forgive me for my thoughtless remark, dear Ashtavakra? I have always loved you as a brother. I do not know what happened to me at that moment.' Then he turned to Uddalak. 'Father, with your permission, may I accompany Ashtavakra on his quest?'

Uddalak smiled. 'You have my permission, son, and both of you have my blessings. Go and humble this arrogant man!'

Both the boys prostrated themselves at Uddalak's feet and embraced Sujata. Then they set off for King Janak's court.

But when they arrived at the palace, the gatekeeper stopped the two simply dressed boys. 'Who are you? What business can you young lads have with the great King Janak?'

'We have come to take part in the shastrartha with Bandin,' Ashtavakra said.

The gatekeeper laughed heartily. 'You, with a twisted body, wish to take part in the shastrartha! Do you even know what it's all about?'

'Do not judge a man by his appearance or his age,' Ashtavakra said. 'We are disciples of the mighty Rishi Uddalak and well-versed in all the branches of learning. We may be young in years but we have more knowledge than most adults. Go tell the king that I have come to challenge Bandin.'

Impressed by the boy's confidence, the gatekeeper went to the king.

King Janak was also surprised to set eyes on this young contender. Being no mean scholar himself, he decided to test Ashtavakra by posing some cryptic questions. When Ashtavakra answered them all without faltering even once, Janak decided that the boy was quite capable of facing Bandin.

But when the two opponents arrived at their seats, the spectators began to laugh when they saw that a young and deformed boy had thrown the gauntlet before Bandin. Ashtavakra was furious. He turned to the king and said, 'Is this supposed to be a gathering of learned men? They are behaving like ignorant people who assess a man more by his appearance and not by the knowledge he possesses.'

Immediately a hush fell over the assembly and the king asked the scholars to begin. Bandin initiated the debate. The contest was to compose verses based on numbers on the spot. Turn by turn, the two were able to create verses on the numbers one to twelve with comparative ease. Then, when they came to the number thirteen, and it was Bandin's turn, the great sage could only come up with the first half of a verse. Seeing that he was stuck, Ashtavakra immediately jumped into the fray and completed the verse effortlessly.

Bandin was thus vanquished, and according to the conditions laid down, he had to grant the victor any wish he desired. Ashtavakra demanded that Bandin be subjected to the same fate as the one he had imposed on the sages he defeated.

Bandin startled all by saying, 'You are welcome to seek this wish, young Ashtavakra. But there is something I have to tell you. I am the son of Varun, the god of water. My father wished to perform a ritual that would require twelve years to complete. He also wanted to get the best rishis to conduct this ceremony. He decided to send me to earth and compel them to enter his world of water by losing to me in a spiritual discussion. Twelve years have now passed and your father will soon be returning. Let us go to the river where he was seen last.'

Both King Janak and Ashtavakra were astounded. The news spread like wildfire and a large crowd of people from the city accompanied them to the river. At the banks of the river, Bandin requested his father to let the rishis go if his ritual had been completed.

Sure enough, all the sages who had supposedly lost their lives emerged from the river, hale and hearty, Kahola among them. Ashtavakra was overjoyed to be reunited with his father and received much praise from all the rishis.

'I am proud to have a son like you!' Kahola said, embracing him. 'Now I declare openly that you are far more intelligent than me. I wish I had not been so short-sighted as to curse you.'

'Now it is time for you to take a dip in the river, Ashtavakra,' Bandin said. 'My father has a special blessing to give you.'

Mystified, Ashtavakra entered the river. When

he came out, the crowd began to shout exultantly. Ashtavakra was no longer crooked in eight places!

After taking leave of King Janak and the others, Kahola returned to the ashram with Ashtavakra and Shvetaketu. Uddalak and Sujata were overjoyed to see them back.

Ashtavakra acquired a reputation for his learning. He returned to Mithila where he became King Janak's guru. He composed the *Ashtavakra Gita* or *Ashtavakra Samhita* as it is sometimes called, a great spiritual treatise.

Hanuman to the Rescue

Ram, the prince of Ayodhya, sprang up and embraced his brother joyously, crying, 'Lakshman! You are alive!' Shouts of jubilation arose from his supporters. It had been an unbearably anxious time and now it seemed the worst was over.

Ram and his army had been fighting Ravan and the forces of Lanka, to rescue his wife Sita whom Ravan had abducted. But their enemy was putting up such a stiff resistance that it looked as if they would have to destroy the ten-headed demon and his whole kingdom to achieve this. Though Ram's cause was the just one, the fortunes of war kept swinging from one side to the other.

In the course of the battle, Lakshman, Ram's younger brother, was critically wounded by Indrajit, Ravan's son. There seemed little hope that he would survive. But luckily, the miraculous sanjeevani herb that the mighty vanar Hanuman brought from the Himalayas, carrying the whole mountain on which it grew, cured him. Lakshman's recovery recharged Ram's followers and they flung themselves enthusiastically into the battle again.

All kinds of weapons were whizzing through the air, many of them powered by divine mantras. Indrajit was targeting Lakshman again, knowing that Ram would be seriously demoralised if his brother perished. When he could make no headway, Indrajit unleashed his most powerful arms—the brahmastra, pashupatastra, and vaishnavastra. But these deadly missiles refused to even touch Lakshman. In fact, the vaishnavastra merely circled Lakshman before disappearing.

The demon prince could not believe his eyes. How could this have happened? Deeply perturbed, he left the battlefield to confer with his father.

'What is the matter, son? Why have you left the battlefield?' Ravan thundered. 'Don't you know we cannot slacken for a moment?'

'I know, Pitashree,' Indrajit said. 'But something extraordinary has happened,' he said. 'I employed my most dangerous weapons against Lakshman, but they did not cause him the slightest harm! I fear we are facing no ordinary mortals, Pitashree. If these potent arms are of no use, how can we hope for victory? The whole of our race could be destroyed by Ram's army. Forgive me for saying this, Pitashree, but it might be prudent to sue for peace and return Sita to her husband.'

An ominous frown appeared on each of Ravan's ten heads. 'Sue for peace? How dare you suggest that?' he bellowed. 'You know very well that we are invincible—I'm ashamed to have fathered a son like you—a coward who has left the battlefield and run back like a dog with his tail between his legs.' He pointed a warning finger at Indrajit. 'Remember this, whatever happens, I will never abandon this fight.'

'I am not a coward, father!' Indrajit shouted back, stung. 'You know that I have been wreaking havoc in the enemy ranks. I had almost finished Lakshman off. If that monkey Hanuman had not brought that herb, Ram's brother would have been in Yama's kingdom by now.' He shook his head angrily, then looked straight at his father. 'And now you doubt my courage! Alright, I will go back and fight to the death. I will show you what I can do, even if you lose me in the bargain!'

His mother Mandodari started up. 'Do not say such things, son!' she cried.

Indrajit did not speak. He simply touched her feet and embraced her. Then he bade goodbye to all his loved ones and returned to the battlefield.

Soon, he was facing Lakshman again. The encounter was ferocious. Both men were armed with a vast variety of weapons, ordinary ones as well as those that had magic powers. Finally, Lakshman flung his indrastra, the celestial missile Lord Indra had given him, at Indrajit. It lopped off the rakshasa's head in one swift blow.

Ram's forces were jubilant. An almost invincible opponent had been felled. This meant they were much closer to rescuing Sita.

When Ravan received the news, he was stunned. For sometime he was overcome with grief, particularly because he had not heeded Indrajit's advice and instead forced him to return to the battle. Then a terrible anger against those responsible for his son's death flared up. He made up his mind to avenge Indrajit. But how could he get even with this powerful enemy, against whom even the unconquerable Indrajit had failed?

He would have to win by trickery.

After a great deal of thought, Ravan summoned his brother Mahiravan who was the king of Patala or the netherworld. 'They have killed my Indrajit!' he cried. 'Our whole rakshasa race is at risk, I fear. You have to help me take revenge, brother.'

One of Ravan's other brothers, Vibhishan, was on Ram's side, knowing his cause was righteous. He managed to learn about the plot Ravan was hatching and warned Ram to be careful.

When he learned this, Hanuman created an impregnable fortress with his tail and placed Ram and Lakshman inside it. But knowing that the rakshasas were well-versed in the dark arts, while the two brothers were resting that night, he stayed on guard. Mahiravan made several attempts to get in, but each time, he could not get past Hanuman. Finally, the rakshasa got a brainwave. He adopted the form of their friend Vibhishan. Hanuman was misled and let him enter. The moment Mahiravan got in, he grabbed hold of the sleeping Ram and Lakshman. Swiftly, he carried them off to his dark kingdom in the depths of the earth.

The rakshasa took them to the temple of his patron goddess Mahamaya and set them down before her image. Ram and Lakshman lay there unconscious and helpless, not knowing where they were and what was happening to them. Mahiravan had laid such a powerful spell on them that there was no way that they could come back to their senses and put up a fight.

Ravan's brother ran a gloating eye over them. 'So you thought you could vanquish us rakshasas?' he asked with a mocking laugh. 'You little know whom you are up against. You may have finished off young Indrajit but we have many more weapons to confound you in our armoury. Right now your army must be in disarray. And before they get even an inkling of your whereabouts, I will have sacrificed you to my deity, the great goddess Mahamaya!'

What Mahiravan did not know was that Hanuman had already discovered that the two brothers were missing. Puzzled, he rushed to Vibhishan.

'Do you know where Ram and Lakshman are?' he asked. 'You were the last person to enter the room. But you didn't come out and they are not there either.'

Vibhishan smote his forehead. 'What are you saying? Alas! It appears that Mahiravan has managed to outwit us. He must have assumed my form to deceive you. He has abducted them, just the way he and Ravan had planned. You will have to act quickly, Hanuman! If you do not save them in time, Mahiravan will sacrifice them to Mahamaya.'

'I should have been more careful!' Hanuman cried, cursing himself. 'But I will go to Patala right away and rescue them. Mahiravan may have outwitted me once, but I'll get even with him this time.'

Hanuman flew to Patala at his fastest speed, faster even than one of the magical arrows that winged so swiftly in the battle. When he reached the gate of the netherworld, he was surprised to find a strange-looking creature standing on guard. The top half of his body was in the shape of a vanar, like Hanuman himself, and the lower half was that of a sea creature.

'Who might you be?' Hanuman asked, gazing at the guard. 'I have never encountered a being like you. You look quite pleased to see me too.'

'I am your son, Makardhwaj!' replied the creature, bowing low and touching his feet. 'O father! How fortunate

I am to meet you at last! What a joyous moment!'

Hanuman was shocked to hear this. 'My son? How can that be?' he frowned. 'I am a brahmachari. Since my youth, I have been strictly celibate. It is not possible that I have a son. Are you trying to fool me?'

'Remember the time when the rakshasas set your tail on fire and you jumped into the ocean to cool off?' said Makardhwaj. 'A drop of your sweat fell into the mouth of a fish. She became pregnant and gave birth to me.'

'Can such a thing happen?' Hanuman asked. 'It is unbelievable. Fortunately I possess the power to verify your story.' He closed his eyes and concentrated hard, trying to summon up the event. This intense dhyan enabled him to arrive at that moment in the past the creature had mentioned. When the scene replayed in his mind, Hanuman found that it had happened exactly as Makardhwaj had described.

'It is true, indeed, it is true!' Hanuman shook his head, wonderstruck. 'An extremely strange thing to happen, but you are right—you are my son. I too am happy to have found you. And now I must ask you to open the gate and let me in. Mahiravan has kidnapped Ram and Lakshman and I have come to rescue them.'

'Now that you have found me, please give me your blessings, father,' Makardhwaj said. 'But I'm afraid I cannot let you in. I have sworn loyalty to my masters. You will have to fight me to enter.'

'You have my blessings, son,' Hanuman said, placing his hand on his son's head. 'And I also understand that you have to do your duty. However, I, too, have sworn loyalty to Ram. It's too bad, but I have to do combat with you.'

Hanuman proceeded to attack Makardhwaj. The fight was over very soon. Hanuman was naturally far stronger. After defeating his son, he tied him up tightly so he could not cause any further trouble by warning his masters.

The mighty vanar then flew into Patal and after a quick look around the place, learnt that Mahiravan was planning to sacrifice Ram and Lakshman to Mahamaya. He realised he would have to get rid of the rakshasa king before he could save the brothers.

Hanuman found Mahiravan and attacked him at once. Mahiravan defended himself. The two mighty warriors grappled with each other for hours. But even Hanuman's immense strength proved ineffective against the demon king. He was taken aback—this had rarely happened.

Hanuman decided to pretend he had given up and retreated. Then he looked for a quiet spot to rest and think of a way to defeat Mahiravan. He knew he had to come up with something quickly. Time was running out. Preparations for the sacrifice had already begun. How could he vanquish the wily Mahiravan?

As he sat there, discarding one scheme after another, he was surprised to find a woman approaching him. She was deeply veiled, but her costly garments made it obvious she was from a very wealthy family. He watched her warily. Who could she be? What did she want from him? When she came close, the woman said in a low voice, 'O Hanuman, I am Chandrasena, Mahiravan's wife. I know you are astonished to see me. You must be wondering what I am doing here, talking with my husband's enemy. But the truth is, I have great respect for the righteous Ram and do not want him to lose his life in this cruel manner. If you will persuade him to look on me with favour, I will tell you how you can defeat my husband.'

'Ram is always favourable towards his devotees,' Hanuman said. 'But you must disclose your secret quickly. There is very little time left before the sacrifice.'

'Alright! The secret of Mahiravan's indestructability lies in the five lamps that burn in the temple,' Chandrasena said. 'If they are blown out at the same time, he will lose his powers. However, the lamps are placed in five different directions, hence it is almost impossible to blow them out at the same time. That is something you will have to work out.'

'I am extremely grateful to you for telling me,' Hanuman said. 'Let us see if it is indeed impossible.'

He thought quickly. Then, using his ability to change shape, Hanuman shrank his frame till he was so small that he was barely visible. He entered the temple undetected, climbed up the image of the goddess and perched on top of it. Though he was tiny, his weight remained the same and he was heavy enough to press the image into the earth. When it had sunk out of sight completely, Hanuman assumed the goddess's form. Barely had he done so than Mahiravan appeared with his entourage to perform the sacrifice.

Ram and Lakshman were still lying there, as motionless as corpses.

Mahiravan made the customary offerings to the goddess, chanting mantras in her praise. Then, he drew his sword and raised it over the two brothers with a loud cry. Just as he was about to bring it down, Hanuman assumed his five-headed or panchmukhi aspect. Since he had acquired victory over his five senses, he possessed the power to do so. The head of Sri Varaha, the boar avatar of Vishnu, faced north, as Sri Narasimha, the lion avatar he faced south, as Sri Garuda, Vishnu's vehicle, he faced west, and as Sri Hayagriva, the horse faced avatar, he looked up at the sky. Hanuman's own face turned towards the east.

With one swift and powerful breath he blew out the five lamps. Then he fell upon the dumbfounded Mahiravan. The rakshasa fought back fiercely but Hanuman overpowered and killed him and decimated his army as well.

No sooner had the rakshsas been destroyed than the spell was broken and Ram and Lakshman regained consciousness. They were astounded to find themselves

in Patala and blessed Hanuman for saving their lives once again.

Patala was without a ruler now, so Ram suggested that Hanuman crown his son Makardhwaj king. Hanuman set Makardhwaj free and the coronation took place with appropriate pomp. After advising Makardhwaj to rule Patala justly and wisely, Hanuman placed the two brothers on his shoulders and brought them back to Lanka.

The battle against Ravan resumed once again. Hanuman had proved that he was Ram's most faithful follower.

The Silent Queen

King Vikramaditya of Ujjain, called Vikram, was one of the wisest and most just monarchs that ever ruled. So concerned was he about the welfare of his subjects that every night he would roam the city in disguise to make sure his people were happy.

One such night he heard a tortured voice crying out, 'Alas, I'll never be able to marry her. It's better to die!'

The startled king saw a knife flash through the darkness. Fearing the worst, he dashed forward and grabbed the man's hand. 'Stop!' he ordered. 'Don't you know it is a sin to take your own life?'

The man turned on him in a rage. 'Who are you to stop me?'

The king showed him his signet ring, saying, 'I am your king. I have vowed that I will make sure no one is unhappy in my kingdom. What is your problem?'

The man, who appeared to be a Brahmin from his appearance, bowed low and said, 'Your majesty, I thank you for your concern, but even the mighty Vikramaditya cannot solve my problem.'

'How can you say that?' King Vikram asked. 'You have not told me what your problem is!'

The man narrated a strange story. 'Your majesty,' he began. 'I have a friend who sells betel leaves for a living. One day a beautiful woman came to his shop and bought one. She flung a coin down in payment and left. When my friend picked it up, he found it was made of gold. He ran after the woman to tell her she had paid him too much but she had vanished in the crowd. The next day she came again and did the same thing. When my friend told her that a betel leaf did not cost so much, she did not reply, just turned and left. She continued to come every day and my friend began to get worried that some trouble might result from this, and confided in me. I decided to follow her secretly to see who she was and where she came from. So, when she left the next day, I pursued her. She walked out of the city into the forest and entered a cave. The cave opened into a fabulous garden. While I stood there wonder-struck, the woman vanished.'

The Brahmin paused for a moment before continuing. 'I must confess that I was not following her for my friend's sake any longer. The truth is, I had lost my heart to her. So I searched frantically in the garden for her and came to a well with a golden wheel. Hearing the sound of voices, I hid. A group of fine-looking women approached the well, carrying golden water pots. '

'"Turn, wheel, in the name of the silent queen," they cried. To my astonishment, the wheel began to turn as if by magic, hauling up water in a golden bucket. They filled their pots and were about to leave when I stopped them. "Beauteous maidens, I beg you to help me!"' I said.

'I told them how I had come there and asked if they knew where I could find that woman. But they said, "It's better that you turn back." "I cannot," I replied. "I have made up my mind that she and none other will be my wife." "Turn back," they repeated. "You will never be able to marry her. She's the silent queen, and will only marry the man who can make her talk."

'"I will make her talk. Just help me to find her,' I begged. 'Better men than you have tried and failed,' they replied, splashing water on my face. I felt faint and fell down. When I came to, I found myself back here in the city ... Your majesty,' he ended, 'if I cannot marry her, I will die.'

'Do not despair,' said King Vikram. 'I will find her and make her marry you.'

This woman is either a supernatural being or well versed in magic, the king thought as he returned to his palace. My wit, strength and courage may not prevail against her. What I need is demon-like cunning, the cunning of the Vetal.

Years earlier, Vikram had been exiled by his brother, King Bhartruhar, who later repented for his unjust actions and left the city. In the absence of a strong ruler, this demon had terrorised Ujjain, demanding that a young man be sent to him each day for food. When Vikram returned from exile, he decided to offer himself to the Vetal to get the better of him.

First, he prepared a wonderful feast. When the Vetal came, he was delighted. He gorged on the food and then said, 'Mortal! You have proved a good host. Before I finish my meal with you as dessert, I will grant you a boon. Ask!'

Vikram replied, 'Well, can you tell me what the exact length of my life is?'

'In a moment!' the Vetal said. He flew off to ask Brahma the creator and returned with the answer. 'One hundred and thirty-five years, seven months, ten days and fifteen minutes,' he said.

'Is that so? Can you extend my life for just one day?' Vikram asked.

The Vetal went again to Brahma, who said, 'The allotted span of a man's life cannot be extended for a second, let alone a day.'

Hearing this, Vikram said, 'Alright, if you can't extend it, ask him to reduce it by one day.' But the Vetal came back with the reply, 'Sorry, Lord Brahma said a man's life cannot be reduced either.'

The moment the demon said this, Vikram sprang forward and grabbed his long hair. 'If you do not have the power to extend or reduce my life, you are making empty threats!' he cried, brandishing his sword. 'You cannot kill me but I will kill you.'

'Spare me!' the demon begged, terrified. 'I have many other powers. Spare me, and I will be your slave forever.'

Vikram spared the Vetal, thinking he could use his help sometime. Now he summoned him from the cremation ground where the demon lived, using the magic words the Vetal had given him.

The night suddenly became darker, and a long swirling shadow appeared. 'What is your command, your majesty?' the Vetal asked, bowing.

Vikram told him about the silent queen and his promise.

'We will make her talk,' the Vetal said. 'I will accompany you in an invisible form.'

The next day the king waited with the Vetal near the betel seller's shop. The woman came as usual, paid with a gold coin and left. Vikram followed her through the forest, into the cave and the garden. And there she vanished.

'An enchantress indeed,' the king murmured. 'But we shall see who prevails.' He set off to search for the well with the golden wheel. He found it and soon the women came to draw water, calling on the wheel to turn in the name of the silent queen.

'Good ladies,' King Vikram said, 'I am looking for the silent queen. I have heard that she will only marry the man who makes her speak. I wish to take up her challenge.'

'Turn back,' said the women, 'if you value your freedom.'

'I have not come this far to turn back,' Vikram replied.

'Alright,' said the tallest of the women. 'But don't say we didn't warn you. Follow us.'

The king found himself sinking into the earth. Then, even as they landed in an open space, piteous cries came to his ears. 'Help! Help us, please!'

To his horror he saw a row of cages before him, each holding a man. 'These unfortunate souls tried to make the silent queen talk and failed,' the tall woman said. 'Do you still want to try?'

'I do,' King Vikram said. 'On the condition that if I succeed, they will be set free.'

'If you succeed!' the woman agreed mockingly. 'Come!'

She led him into a wondrous palace with marble floors and domed ceilings covered with gold leaf. They entered a richly furnished room where King Vikram could dimly glimpse a woman seated behind three screens made of the finest gauze, embroidered with seed pearls.

'If you make her speak once,' the tall woman said,

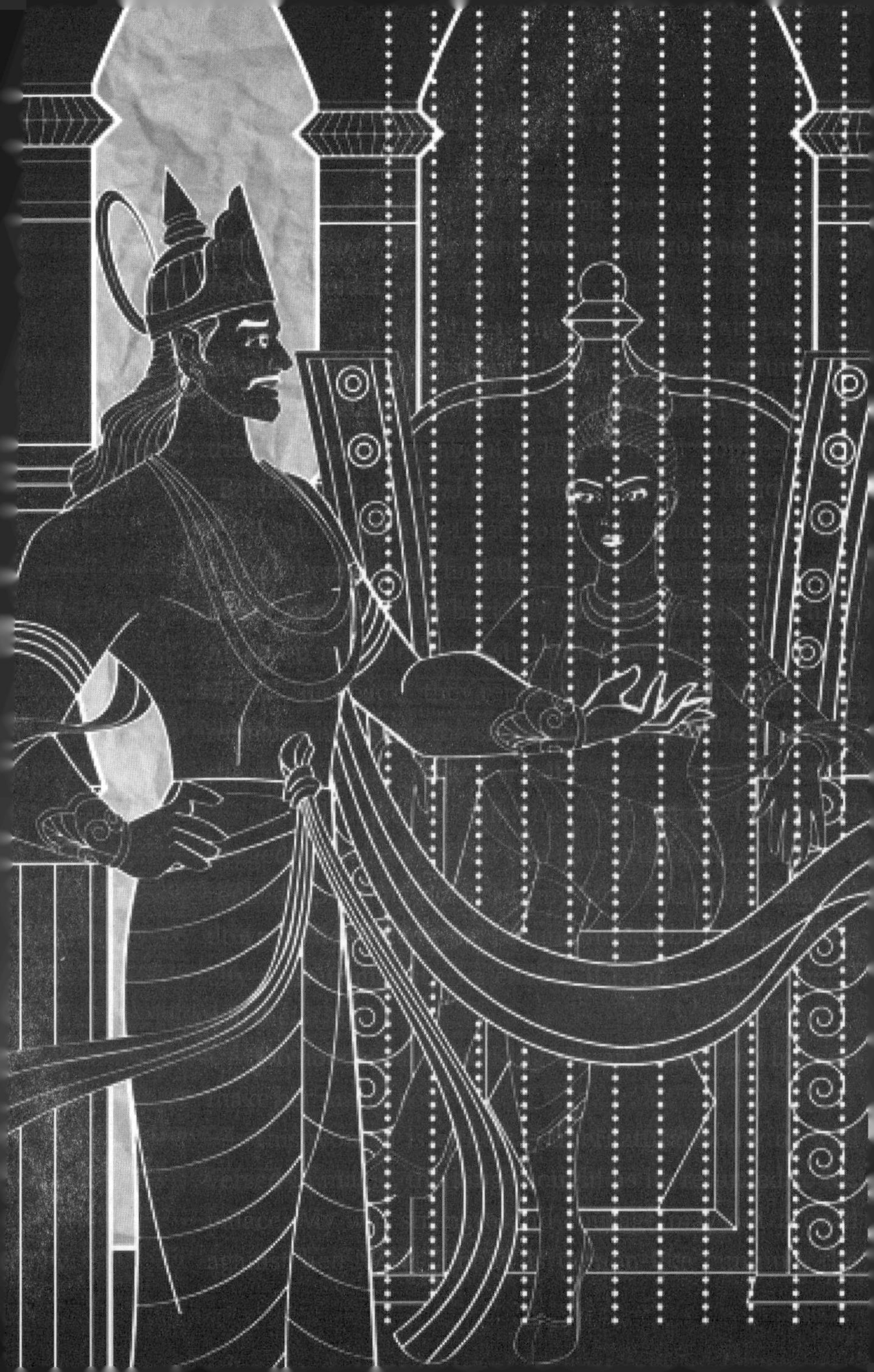

'the first screen will be removed. Twice, the second, and thrice, the last. So you must make her speak three times. But if you fail ... you know what awaits you.'

Vikram nodded indifferently. 'I will tell her a story,' he said, 'and if she doesn't speak, her earring will.'

'Earring!' the tall woman laughed. 'We'll see!'

Vikram silently instructed the Vetal to enter the mute queen's earring. Then he began, 'Once upon a time, there lived four friends, a Brahmin, a carpenter, a goldsmith and a weaver. One day, to amuse themselves, the carpenter made a wooden doll. The weaver made clothes for it, the goldsmith adorned it with jewellery, and finally, the Brahmin brought it to life. But then the four of them began to fight, each saying she was his wife. Now whose wife should she rightly be?' Vikram asked.

The silent queen kept her mouth firmly shut but a voice came from her earring, 'The Brahmin, because he brought her to life.'

At once the queen cried out, 'Not at all! The one who created her is her father, the one who gave her clothes is her brother, the one who gave her life is like God, but the one who gave her ornaments is her husband.'

'You spoke,' Vikram said, smiling. The queen nodded and signalled for the first screen to be removed.

'Now I'll tell you another story,' Vikram said. 'And if you don't speak, your necklace shall.' He began, 'A childless king worshipped Lord Shiva and was blessed with a son. According to custom, the boy was married to a princess as a child. When he grew up, he went to fetch her, accompanied by a friend. On the way, he stopped to offer lotuses at a Shiva temple and promised to do the same on his return. But on his way back with the princess, he couldn't find any lotuses, so he cut off his head and offered it to the god. When he didn't come out of the temple for a long time, his friend went in to look for him. Finding him dead, he was overcome with sorrow and cut his own head off too. The princess waited for a while and when no one returned, she entered the temple. When she found the prince dead, she did not wish to live either, and decided to cut off her head as well. The moment she picked up the sword, Shiva appeared. He told her that he was pleased with their devotion, and would grant her the boon of restoring their lives. She should put the heads back on the bodies, cover them with a cloth and sprinkle water on them. The princess did that, but when they came alive, to her dismay she discovered that she had attached the wrong head to the wrong body. Now she was confronted with the difficult question—who was her real husband?'

Vetal, who had entered the necklace, said, 'The one with the body of the prince is her rightful husband.'

'Wrong!' the silent queen exclaimed. 'It's the head that rules the body, so the one with the prince's head is her husband.'

The second screen was now removed.

'This is the last story I will tell you,' Vikram said, exulting at his success. 'And this time, if you don't speak, your anklet will.' The silent queen shrugged. 'There was once a beautiful princess. When she was old enough, her father arranged for her to marry a prince from a neighbouring country. In the meantime, her brother who was travelling abroad came across another prince who impressed him greatly, and promised his sister in marriage to him. At the same time, her mother who was visiting her own father found another suitable match for the princess. Now all three suitors arrived to marry her and when they discovered what had happened, they began to fight amongst themselves. While they were quarrelling, the princess was bitten by a snake and died. All three mourned her. One scattered her ashes in the river Ganga, one went on a pilgrimage, and the third sat and worshipped her bones. Now the one who went on pilgrimage learned the art of bringing the dead back to life. He returned quickly and revived the princess. But when he did, the three suitors began to quarrel again. Who do you think should marry her?' King Vikram asked.

The queen remained silent, but another voice spoke. 'Naturally, the one who brought her to life,' her anklet jingled.

'Certainly not!' the queen protested. 'The one who

gave her another birth is her father, the one who dispersed the ashes is her son, but the one who sat and worshipped her bones is her true husband.'

'You spoke for the third time!' Vikram cried out.

'You are right,' said the silent queen, emerging from behind the last screen. 'I accept you as a husband worthy of me because of your wit and wisdom.' She held out her hand.

King Vikram bowed low but did not take her hand. 'I have a final question for you,' he said. 'If a king undertakes a task on behalf of one of his subjects, who should receive the reward?'

'The subject, of course,' said the queen, without a second thought. 'He is not acting on his own behalf.'

'I bow to your wisdom,' King Vikram said. 'I am King Vikramaditya of Ujjain. I took up your challenge on behalf of one of my subjects, a young man who was ready to die for your sake. I request that you marry him and free those unfortunate men.'

'Who can refuse the just King Vikramaditya?' said the queen with a smile.

While she ordered her attendants to open the cages, Vikram signalled to Vetal that he was free to return to his dwelling place until he should be needed again.

Vikram went back to the city with the silent queen. She married the young Brahmin with much festivity and they lived happily in the kingdom of the just King Vikram.

Bhim and the Monkey

The five Pandavs and their cousins, the hundred Kauravs, were fighting for the throne of Hastinapur. By right, Yudhishtir, the eldest among both the Pandavs and Kauravs, should have been crowned, but the Kauravs kept plotting to prevent him. After many of their plans did not work, Duryodhan, the oldest Kaurav, invited him to a game of dice. Yudhishtir lost everything he possessed in this game and was forced to agree to go into exile with his brothers for twelve years. There was a further condition. In the thirteenth year, the Pandavs were to live in disguise, and if they were discovered, they would have to stay banished for another thirteen years.

When the sixth year of this punishment began, Arjun left his family to perform a penance to please Lord Shiva and acquire invincible weapons.

His brothers and their wife Draupadi all missed

him terribly. And when just two years of banishment remained, they travelled to the Himalayas and began to live at an ashram known as Badri and waited for Arjun to join them there.

It was a most charming spot, filled with the twitter of birdsong. The most unusual flowers bloomed there too. One day, as Draupadi was seated outside, enjoying the lovely view of the mountains, the wind blew a beautiful flower towards her. She picked it up wonderingly and an enchanting perfume filled her nostrils. So enchanting that she could not let go of the flower and simply sat there holding it in her hand and inhaling its fragrance over and over again.

After a while, Bhim came out of the ashram. Immediately, she showed it to him, saying, 'Isn't this a gorgeous flower? And so sweetly scented! It's a saugandhika, I think. How I would love to have more of these! Can you get some for me?'

'If you are so captivated by this flower, I'll get more for you right away,' Bhim replied.

He set off through the forest following the trail of perfume that the wind had spread. He went on and on, but did not find these flowers growing anywhere. Soon he had ventured so far that he could not even guess where he was. So he decided to blow his conch as loud as he could in case there was someone in the forest who could guide him. But the only response he got was an echo from the mountain in front of him. Wondering how he would get back, he went a little further.

As he walked, he came across a huge monkey sitting on the path blocking his way, and was forced to halt.

'Who are you, young man?' the monkey asked. 'Why are you making such a noise? Do you know you woke me up from my sleep? And where do you think you're going? Let me give you some advice. You will not be able to go any further. Here, have some fruit and turn back.'

Bhim was surprised to find the monkey speaking, and a little annoyed that he was telling him to turn back. He replied politely, 'May I ask who you are, good sir? You don't seem to be an ordinary monkey. Thank you for your kind advice, but I do not intend to turn back. I am going to search for some saugandhika flowers for my dear wife Draupadi. Will you kindly move out of my way?'

'I'm too old to move, my dear young man. If you wish to go on, you will have to jump over me.'

'How can I be so disrespectful as to jump over an elder?' Bhim asked angrily. 'But if you insist, I can very well jump over you like the mighty Hanuman jumped over the sea.'

'Who is this Hanuman you're talking about?' asked the monkey with a mocking smile. 'You seem to think very highly of him.'

Bhim was really disgusted now. 'What kind of a monkey are you that you don't even know who the mighty Hanuman is? He is the greatest of all monkeys, the ardent devotee of Lord Ram. Don't you know about all the feats he performed in Ram's service? He happens to be my brother. We are both sons of Vayu, the god of wind. And I am Bhim, one of the five Pandavs, the sons of Kunti. We have been sent into exile and are waiting for our brother Arjun to rejoin us here. If you don't move aside now, I will have to force you to move. I may not be as powerful as Hanuman but I am strong enough to tackle a monkey, even one as gigantic as you.'

The monkey smiled again. 'Why are you getting so upset, young man?' he asked. 'I really am too old to move. It's my tail that's blocking the path. Why don't you just push it aside and go on?'

'Alright,' Bhim said. 'That's very easily done.'

He bent and tried to flick the monkey's tail aside with his left hand. But the tail did not budge even an inch. Puzzled, Bhim now used both his hands and shoved with all his might. However, once again, he could not move the monkey's tail. Bhim was really disturbed now. How was it possible that he, the mighty Bhim, was unable to displace something as ordinary as an old monkey's tail?

He tried once more. Perspiration streamed down his body as he used the full force of his huge muscles. But still the monkey's tail lay there rooted like a rock.

At last he realised that moving the tail was an impossible task. Humiliated and ashamed, he bowed to the ground before the monkey and said, 'Please forgive me. I have behaved very discourteously towards you. You are obviously someone very great. Will you tell me who you are, respected sir?'

The monkey smiled kindly. 'I too am keen to tell you who I am. Like you, I am the son of Vayu. I am Hanuman.'

'Hanuman!' Overjoyed, Bhim rushed to embrace his brother.

Now that they had found each other, the brothers did not want to part. They talked for a long time. 'I came here to warn you that the path ahead is not safe,' Hanuman said. 'But I can't tell you how proud I am that you are so strong and brave. I want to grant you a boon in memory of this meeting.'

Bhim's voice turned serious. 'Dear brother, as you know, a crucial fight lies before us. All I ask for is your support in our battle for our rights against the Kauravs,' he said.

'Be assured, brother,' Hanuman replied, patting his head. 'I will be there, sitting on the staff of Arjun's banner. My voice will join yours when you roar like a lion on the battlefield, striking terror in the hearts of your enemies.'

Bhim bowed low at his feet and said, 'Then we have nothing to fear. But ... I have one request,' he ended hesitantly.

'What is it?' Hanuman asked. 'I will happily fulfil whatever you ask.'

'I have always been intrigued by the story of the mighty form you assumed when you jumped over the sea to reach Lanka,' Bhim said with folded hands. 'Please, could you grant me a vision of it?'

'Certainly,' Hanuman replied.

Bhim watched wide-eyed as Hanuman grew larger and larger till he seemed to occupy all the space around them. Overcome with awe, Bhim bowed low before this wondrous aspect of his brother. 'You have granted me an unforgettable revelation. For this I thank you, my brother.'

Hanuman shrank back to his normal size and enfolded Bhim in his arms.

Bhim's strength increased hugely after this embrace. Then Hanuman told him the way to the river where the saugandhika flowers grew. Bhim had to battle many rakshasas to pluck the flowers, since they belonged to Kuber, the god of wealth. But when Kuber found out that it was Bhim who wanted the flowers, he let him take as many as he wanted.

Bhim bore the flowers back to Draupadi, who was

waiting anxiously. He shared the story of his encounter with Hanuman with his brothers. They were greatly cheered and felt it boded well for the future.

Hanuman did place himself on Arjun's banner when the battle of Kurukshetra took place, and his presence added greatly to their morale in that terrible struggle.

The Adventures of Kirtisena

In the ancient city of Pataliputra, there lived a wealthy merchant named Dhanpalit. Dhanpalit had only one child, a daughter named Kirtisena. She was not only beautiful but intelligent as well, and her father doted on her. When Kirtisena grew old enough to get married, he looked around for a suitable match. He found one equal to her in merit, a merchant of Magadha named Devasena. The wedding was celebrated with much pomp and show and Kirtisena went to live with her husband's family.

Now Devasena was a gentle and good-natured man and treated his wife with much love and affection. His mother, on the other hand, was as ill-tempered and as sharp-tongued as it was possible for a woman to be. However, she was clever enough to save her nasty behaviour for the times when Devasena was not around. And Kirtisena was too devoted to her husband to complain about his mother to him.

Then one day, Devasena announced that he had decided to go to a distant place, Valabhi, to trade with his fellow merchants. When Kirtisena heard this, she was overcome with fear.

'I understand you have to travel on business and will be gone for a long time. But I am mortally afraid to stay here without you,' she told her husband. 'I kept this to myself all this time ... but the truth is, your mother treats me most cruelly when you are not present. If you go away on such a long journey, I don't know what my fate will be.'

While Devasena cared a great deal for his wife, he also respected his mother. He decided to appeal to her better side. He went to her and said in his most loving tone, 'Ma, I have a request. As you know, I am travelling to distant lands. In my absence, please treat Kirtisena kindly. She has been brought up with much love by her father and is easily hurt. Try and control your tongue when you speak to her.' This angered his mother even more. 'So the two-faced creature is trying to turn you against me!' she screamed. 'When have I addressed any but the kindest words to her? God knows I have always treated her like my own daughter.'

Devasena remained silent. He was well aware that his mother had a foul temper but as a dutiful son, he did not want to get into an argument with her. Listening to this exchange, Kirtisena became even more terrified. However, she did not want her husband to get anxious, so she tried to look cheerful as she bade him goodbye.

The consequences were just what she had expected. The moment her husband left, his mother began to wreak vengeance for her having dared to complain about her. She turned out all the servants except one elderly maid who was her ally in whatever she did. Together the two of them beat Kirtisena till she was almost senseless. Then they both pushed her into an underground cellar. Kirtisena was held prisoner there and given only a handful of rice per day to eat. Her mother-in-law hoped to finish her off by slow starvation and planned to tell her son that his wife had run away.

For a few days, Kirtisena lay there, numb with despair. Then, as she recalled Devasena's love for her and the happy times they had spent together, she decided she would not give up and let her evil mother-in-law win. Somehow she had to save herself. But how could she escape from the cellar? She began to think of possible ways and searched for tools that might help her to get out. As she was groping about in the cellar one day, she came across an iron rod. Hope spurted in her heart.

Perhaps she could dig her way out of there!

By now Kirtisena had become extremely weak. But she knew this was her only chance. So she pulled herself together and devoted all her energy to excavating a tunnel. She worked mostly at night when she knew everyone was fast asleep and tried to make as little sound as she could. It was an extremely tough job, trying to bore through the hard earth and do it without anyone noticing. Luckily her mother-in-law had become quite complacent, believing her scheme was succeeding and her daughter-in-law was already half dead out of starvation. The possibility that she might attempt to escape never occurred to her.

After labouring for several days, the iron rod broke free of the ground. A gust of fresh air came to Kirtisena. She breathed it in deeply. Overjoyed and greatly encouraged, she laboured with all the strength that remained in her fragile frame. Soon the tunnel was large enough for her to wriggle through.

But she would need some clothes and money. Though the prospect of being caught was terrifying, she gathered together all her courage and tiptoed into her own room while her mother-in-law slept, to collect her husband and her own clothes and some jewellery. After that she crept out again and ran through the silent streets of the city to get as far from her house as she could.

But where was she to go now? Kirtisena did not wish to make her father unhappy by going to his house and telling him about her troubles. She decided to search for her husband instead. Slowly, she walked out of the city. Just outside the walls, she found a pond. There she bathed and dressed herself in men's garments. She rested for a while and when morning came, she headed to the city again and sold some of her jewels. Thus she got enough money to support herself for the time-being. She found a place to stay at an inn and kept her ears open for news of anyone travelling towards her husband's destination. After a few days, she heard that a group of merchants were going to Valabhi. She dressed herself in her husband's finest clothes and jewellery. Then, posing as a prince, she approached them and asked if she could accompany them.

To avoid paying taxes, the merchants decided to journey through the forest instead of taking the regular route. They were well-armed and felt they could face any danger that might befall them. On their way, they reached an area which was infested with dacoits. Hearing the men talk about it, Kirtisena was overcome with dread. If dacoits attacked, they would be caught and she might be exposed as a woman. No sooner had these thoughts flashed through her mind than fierce cries rang out through the air.

It was dacoits attacking!

Kirtisena wasted no time fleeing from the scene. As luck would have it, she found a dense grove of trees nearby and managed to hide inside it. The merchants battled the dacoits with all their might but were outnumbered and killed. The dacoits plundered their goods and went their way, not suspecting that another member of the group was concealed nearby.

When day came, Kirtisena took to the road again. She had no idea where it led, but fortunately she came across a holy man. He gave her a much-needed drink of water and told her how to reach Valabhi. Kirtisena walked all through the day and satisfied her hunger with berries and wild fruit growing in the forest. When night fell she was able to find a huge hollow tree to sleep in, where she would be safe from wild animals. Now while Kirtisena lay in the hollow, an ogress passed that way with her children. She stopped right beneath this tree. Kirtisena felt her blood turn to ice as she heard the children say, 'Ma, we're very hungry. Get us something to eat.'

'Have patience, my dears,' the ogress replied. 'I will get you lots of food soon. I had gone to the cremation ground and could not find a single corpse to feed on. But I was told that the king of Vasuduttpur is on his death bed. He had come to hunt in the forest and as he lay asleep under a tree, an earwig entered his ear. It laid eggs inside his head and the king had fallen terribly sick. So far no vaidya has been able to diagnose his ailment and cure him.'

'But Ma,' the children said, 'suppose some vaidya does manage to cure him before we reach there?'

'There is no chance of that,' said the rakshasi. 'Because there is only one way to cure him, which no one knows about. They should rub warm ghee on his head and make him lie in the sun. Then they should put a bamboo pipe in his ear. This pipe must lead into a clay vessel of water. The heat will drive the insects out towards the water. But not a single person has any idea about this method. The king's death is as sure and certain as we are standing here, my dears.'

Kirtisena had been listening with bated breath. She decided that if she was able to get out of the forest alive, she would go to Vasuduttpur and save the king's life.

Next morning, after the rakshasi and her children went their way, Kirtisena managed to gather the courage to climb out of the hollow tree. She set off down the forest path and met a milkman on the way. He happened to be going to Vasuduttpur too and was able to tell her how to get to the palace. When she reached there, Kirtisena presented herself as a learned vaidya. She was taken to the king who lay on his bed moaning and groaning in terrible pain.

Kirtisena did exactly as the rakshasi had suggested. She rubbed warm ghee on the king's head and made him lie in the sun. Then she attached a bamboo pipe to his ear and put the other end in a vessel of water. His attendants and courtiers were astounded to find hundreds of insects come pouring out of his ear.

The pain vanished and the king began to feel much better the very next day. Overjoyed, he rewarded Kirtisena with a lot of gold and jewels, and many horses and elephants. He even requested her to settle down in the city. Kirtisena began to live there, still disguised as a man. But all the time she was longing to find her husband. Whenever she came across groups of travelling merchants, she would ask them if they had heard of a man named Devasena. Finally her efforts bore fruit. One day she learned that a merchant from Magadh called Devasena was expected in Vasuduttpur.

The moment Kirtisena got the news that Devasena had arrived, she set off to meet him at the inn where he was staying. When Devasena set eyes on his wife, he recognised her at once, in spite of her male attire. 'But what are you doing here?' he asked.

Kirtisena's face fell. She told him the whole story—why she was compelled to run away from home.

Devasena became grim. 'It is entirely my fault,' he said with a sigh. 'I should have realised how serious the situation was. What can I say, Kirtisena, but beg for your forgiveness? And as for your courage ... no amount of praise will be enough.'

'It was the memories of our happy life together that

gave me the strength to do it,' Kirtisena said, wiping away her tears.

Now Kirtisena could cast off the men's clothes she had been wearing for such a long time. Everyone was astonished to discover that she actually was a woman. The king, who remained eternally grateful to her, said that since she had brought him back to life, he considered her his sister.

Devasena and Kirtisena decided to settle down at Vasuduttpur and were always treated with great honour by the king.

The Boy Who Defeated Death

A sage named Mrikandu and his wife Marudwati lived in their ashram in the forest. They were a god-fearing couple, mostly content with what they had, but they were unhappy that they lacked one important thing in their lives—a child. After waiting for many years, they decided to visit all the holy places and offer prayers so that they may be blessed with a child. They went everywhere on pilgrimage and finally reached Kedarnath. However, in spite of their sincere prayers, they were not rewarded with any children. Disappointed and downcast, they returned to the forest and decided to spend their lives in prayer and fasting till they died.

The sight of the young animals frisking about would fill Marudwati with an unbearable longing for a baby of her own. One day, while she went to fetch water from the river, she met a woman in whom she confided her sorrow. She advised her to pray to Shiva. Both Mrikandu and Marudwati began to worship Shiva. Touched by the depth of their desire and their heartfelt prayers, one day the god himself appeared to them. Mrikandu and Marudwati were overcome and fell at his feet. But what Lord Shiva said put them in a quandary. He told them he would bless them with a son but they would have to choose. Would they prefer a god-fearing child who had a short life, or one who would live long but be irreligious? Without a moment's hesitation, the couple asked for the former.

At last a son was born to them. At the moment of his birth, a voice spoke from the sky, 'This child will live only till the age of twelve!' The couple were distraught to hear this but finally decided that whatever happened, it was god's will. They devoted themselves to bringing up the boy, whom they named Markandeya.

When Markandeya reached the age of five, his parents sent him to a gurukul to study. He was an exemplary scholar, a lad who dedicated himself to his studies and to serving his guru. He was so good-natured that everyone in the gurukul loved him. Markandeya was extremely pious too. When the other students were playing or simply resting, he would be meditating or be deep in prayer. By the age of eleven, he acquired all the knowledge he could, and his guru sent him home with his blessings.

His parents were overjoyed to have him back. But the thought that he had only one more year to live plunged them into gloom. The sensitive Markandeya could not help noticing that their eyes were always anxious when they looked at him. He had never seen them smile or laugh since he had returned, and often caught his mother in tears.

Disturbed, one day Markandeya asked his father, 'Pitashree, you and my respected mother seem to be very sad about something. Please could you share the reason with me? Even though I am a child, perhaps I can help to relieve your sorrow.'

His father replied with a long sigh, 'My son, I never wanted to tell you, but the fact is, you do not have long to live. It was destined, when you were born, that you would survive only till the age of twelve. This is why our eyes are always brimming with tears. You should spend your spare time in prayer and worship.'

Markandeya was silent for a moment, then he said, 'Please do not worry, Pitashree. Wait and see, I will earn a long life for myself through the power of my prayers.' Even as he spoke, Narad muni, the well-known sage, appeared.

'I heard what you said, Markandeya,' he said. 'It is

next to impossible to reverse what fate has decreed, but the human will can sometimes work wonders. Why don't you go to the banks of the river Gautami and pray to Shiva? Repeat the mantra "Om Namoh Shivaya!" constantly.'

Markandeya's parents sent him off with a heavy heart. The lad reached the banks of the river, made a shivalinga out of sand and began to pray to it. Narad, who was fond of creating controversy, went off to visit Yamaraj and informed him that young Markandeya was engaged in a rigorous penance to defeat him.

Yamaraj was not affected at all by this piece of information. 'It will be of no use,' he said. 'No one can escape death, no matter how hard he tries.'

'I suppose you are the best judge of that,' Narad said with a shrug, and went his way. But Yamaraj had received a warning.

Markandeya continued to pray day and night. The seasons changed, the shrubs and other plants grew denser and denser around him, but immersed in his worship, he did not notice anything. The animals would stand and watch him at his penance, amazed at his perseverance.

It so happened that the seven rishis, Vashishth, Kashyap, Atri, Bharadwaj, Vishwamitra, Gautam and Jamadagni passed that way. They were highly impressed with Markandeya's single-mindedness. 'Who is this bright-faced child?' asked Vashishth.

Markandeya bowed to them and said, 'I am Markandeya, respected rishis.'

'May you live long!' All the seven sages raised their hands to grant him the customary blessings for a long life given to the young.

But Markandeya replied, 'I thank you greatly, respected sages, but the days of my existence are almost over. That is why I am engaged in penance.'

When they heard that, the rishis were shocked. 'It is highly unjust that one so promising should be doomed to an early death!' they exclaimed. 'We will go to Brahma himself and ask him to grant you a long life.'

However, when they went to Brahma, he said, 'Shiva is the only one who can save Markandeya.'

Perturbed, but not willing to give up, the sages returned and taught Markandeya the *mahamrityunjaya strotra*, the mantra that is said to have power over death itself. Markandeya began to repeat that prayer. At the same time, his parents, too, were praying earnestly for a longer life to be granted to their son. Seeing that the gods were so pleased with Markandeya's single-minded devotion, Yamaraj began to get worried.

Time continued to pass and the day predicted for Markandeya's death, his twelfth birthday, drew nearer and nearer. Finally it arrived.

Yamaraj sent his messengers to bring Markandeya

to the land of the dead. But when they reached him, they could not approach. The radiance he had acquired by the power of his penance was so dazzling that it was impossible for them to keep their eyes open in his presence. They returned to Yama with heads bowed low in shame and confessed their inability to fetch Markandeya.

Yamaraj scolded them roundly. 'What kind of messengers are you that a twelve-year-old boy can overpower you?' he asked. 'It looks like I will have to go and get him myself.'

At that very moment, who should arrive but Narad muni! 'This is your test,' he told Yamaraj mockingly. 'Let's see if you are up to the challenge!'

'No one can defeat death,' said Yamaraj calmly, 'even the greatest, the most pious of men. It is one of the inescapable realities of human existence.'

'This boy's staunch prayers are also an inescapable reality,' Narad replied with a smile.

'I'll see about that!' Yama shrugged. He mounted his buffalo and set off, carrying his noose.

He found Markandeya by the river. 'Come along, boy,' he said, 'your time is up.'

'Wait, Yamaraj,' said Markandeya. 'My puja is not complete. I still have to offer rice to Lord Shiva.'

Yama laughed loudly. 'Death does not wait for anyone,' he said.

'Alright,' Markandeya replied. 'You do your work, I'll do mine.'

'O Shiva, you granted me as a boon to my parents,' Markandeya prayed. 'I offer my body to you as the rice of my worship.'

He embraced the shivalinga tightly. At that very moment, Yamaraj flung his noose around his neck. However, even as he did, the noose encircled the shivalinga as well.

'Give up, boy!' Yamaraj cried, pulling at the noose. 'I've got you now!'

A great tremor went through the earth, and even the highest of mountains shook. The birds began to fly around wildly in panic and the animals rushed about in alarm.

Yamaraj felt the force of the earthquake too, and was taken aback. As he stood there mystified, Shiva appeared from the linga in a fury. He pushed Yamaraj away with all his might and was about to destroy him. Terrified, the god of death pleaded for mercy. But Shiva's anger would not be appeased.

Overcome with anxiety, all the gods appeared and begged Shiva to spare Yama. 'The whole cycle of nature will end if Yamaraj is destroyed,' they said.

Shiva relented at last. Then he told Markandeya to ask for a boon.'

'All I ask is to be your eternal devotee, lord,' said the boy.

Shiva granted Markandeya the boon of immortality. At that very moment his apprehensive parents arrived on the scene. They were ecstatic when they found that their son had been saved from death and could not thank Shiva enough.

Markandeya led a long life filled with prayer and good deeds. He devoted himself to spreading knowledge and helping others.

Sixteen Pots of Gold

A forlorn-looking woman was sitting by the side of the road that led out of the ancient city of Mithila, when a man passed by driving his cart.

She sprang to her feet immediately and asked, 'Kind sir, will you be going as far as Kalachampa?'

The man's eyes opened wide in surprise. The woman was poorly dressed, but from her refined speech, she sounded like a woman of noble birth. However, he did not question her, and taking pity on her plight, asked her to get on to the cart. When they reached the city, the man dropped her off by a temple and went his way.

The woman sat outside the temple looking dejected and confused as if she did not know what to do next and where to go. A Brahmin teacher happened to pass that way with his pupils. Noticing that she looked troubled, he stopped to ask her if he could help her in any way.

The woman told him a sad story. She said that she was the former queen of Mithila and her husband King Aritthajanak had been killed in battle by his enemy Poljanak. She had fled to save her own life as well as that of her unborn child.

Touched by her sad situation, the Brahmin offered her shelter in his own home. He introduced her to his wife as his sister who had come from a far-off place after losing her husband. When her time came, the queen gave birth to a son whom she named Mahajanak. The Brahmin and his wife took good care of her and her child grew up in their home.

Mahajanak turned out to be a strong and healthy lad. One day, while playing with the neighbourhood boys, he got into a quarrel with one of them and beat him up.

In retaliation, the boy said, 'Wait and see, I will tell my father. He'll take care of you.'

Mahajanak replied, 'I will tell mine too.'

When he said this, all the boys burst out laughing. 'Tell your father? You have no father,' they mocked. 'Who will you tell?'

Humiliated, Mahajanak ran to his mother in tears. She consoled him and said, 'That's not true. You had a father, a man far greater than any of our neighbours. He was the king of Mithila. Unfortunately, he was killed by his enemies. I had to flee Mithila with just a few jewels to save my life and yours.' Wiping her eyes, she continued, 'If your kind uncle and aunt had not given me refuge, I don't know what would have become of us.'

'Is that so, mother?' Mahajanak's eyes gleamed with excitement. 'Why didn't you tell me earlier? I would have settled all those fools.'

'No, no, son! This is one secret we cannot disclose!' his mother cried anxiously. 'You are still very young. If word reaches our enemies' ears, they will lose no time in finishing us off.'

Mahajanak immediately became serious. 'I will not let a whisper of this get out, mother,' he said.

A great change came over Mahajanak from that day. He stopped being playful and devoted himself to his studies, preparing himself to be the ruler of Mithila one day.

He grew into a tall and strong young man and it warmed his mother's heart to see him. One day he asked her, 'Do you have any money to spare? I think it is time I went to Mithila and reclaimed my throne.'

'I do. I took care to save what I could,' his mother replied, embracing him joyfully. 'O son, I have long been waiting for this day.' She took out the jewellery and gold coins that remained with her and handed them to him. But Mahajanak took only half of them, saying, 'Save the rest, mother. I will use this to earn more.'

He joined a group of merchants and set off to trade overseas to raise the money he would need to gather an army.

At the same time as Mahajanak left on his journey, Poljanak, the man who had usurped his father's throne, lay on his deathbed. He had no sons, only an intelligent and beautiful daughter named Shivali. Concerned about her future, Poljanak instructed his ministers to place the man his daughter chose as her husband on the throne. However, he would first have to fulfil certain conditions that Poljanak listed for them, to prove that he was fit to rule the country.

First, he would have to point out the head of the princess' square bed. Then, he would have to string a mighty bow that required the strength of a hundred men to perform this task. Finally, he would have to locate the treasure placed in the sixteen pots of gold that the king had hidden around the palace. Poljanak provided sixteen clues to help in the treasure hunt.

Barely had he passed on these directions than the king's breath began to falter. And before the day ended, he passed away. The ministers were left with the difficult task of finding a suitable husband for the princess and a monarch for the country. They decided to search among the people they knew first.

The general of the king's army was young, brave and handsome. The ministers believed he might be the right person. So they approached the princess with their views about the general as a possible husband for her.

'Tell him to come and see me at once,' she said.

The general was overwhelmed with joy when he heard that the princess had summoned him. Eager not to keep her waiting, he ran up the stairs that led to her chamber as fast as he could. The princess, who was watching, was not at all impressed by this. His behaviour demonstrated a lack of poise and dignity, she felt.

When the general appeared before her, he bowed low and said, 'Your highness, if I am chosen, I vow I will always be at your service. No task you ask me to perform will be too menial for me, if it pleases you.'

'Hmm ...' said the princess. 'Then you are not the right husband for me. You are too servile.' She sent the general away.

The ministers put their heads together again and decided on the treasurer, a man who was both wise and good-looking. But he too failed to win the princess over. So did all the other suitors who lined up to woo her.

At this time Mahajanak was on board a ship that was carrying him and his merchandise to a far-off land. A severe storm suddenly broke out and the ship, battered by the waves, fell apart. Mahajanak held on tight to the mast and was washed ashore. He did not know it, but he had reached the state of Mithila.

He entered the city and while he rested in a garden,

he overheard two men talking. Only then did he realise where the storm had carried him. He also discovered from their conversation that Mithila was without a king. This filled him with hope and renewed his enthusiasm, even though he had lost all his money and goods in the storm and did not have the means to raise an army and assert his right.

The ministers were in a real quandary now. It was dangerous for the state to remain without a king for too long. Enemy rulers were likely to be tempted to attack and conquer the kingdom. Finally, they asked the royal priest for advice. The priest suggested that they send out the sacred chariot of Mithila.

'In the past, whenever a difficult decision had to be made, this chariot was driven through the streets of the city,' he said. 'It has never failed to provide the correct answer. I'm sure it will lead us to the right man.'

The sacred chariot was brought out of the stables, and cleaned and polished. Horses were harnessed to it and the charioteer set off. The ministers followed, along with a crowd of eager citizens, as it sped through the streets of Mithila. Suddenly, as if guided by an unseen force, the horses speeded up and turned towards a garden. They stopped directly in front of Mahajanak, who lay there fast asleep. Everyone was astonished that the chariot had chosen a complete stranger. Since Mahajanak was sleeping, the priest suggested that the musicians in the entourage beat drums and blow horns to observe his reaction when he awoke. Hearing the noise, Mahajanak opened his eyes, and then closed them again. He would learn the reason for this din sooner or later, he thought. There was no point in getting worked up about it.

'What a man!' exclaimed the prime minister. 'In spite of the terrible racket, he remains cool and composed. Most people would be thrown into a panic.'

'I told you the chariot would find an answer,' said the priest. He approached Mahajanak. 'Good sir,' he said, 'you seem to be a stranger to this land. Our king passed away recently, leaving behind an unmarried daughter. He left instructions for his ministers to find a suitable match for her—a man who will have to pass certain tests to prove himself worthy. Our king considered these essential since her husband will also occupy the throne of Mithila. I am the royal priest and wish to ask if you will agree to be a suitor for the hand of the princess and prospective ruler of our country.'

Mahajanak rose in a leisurely manner and said, 'Alright. I agree.'

Mahajanak was then seated in a chariot and brought to the palace. When the princess heard that the chariot had chosen a stranger, she was eager to test him. She sent a maid asking him to come and meet her at once. But on receiving the message, Mahajanak did not respond right away. Neither did he get up when she sent the message again. Only when she called him the third time did he rise and proceed towards the princess' chamber. Even so, he walked at a slow and easy pace. The princess was impressed by his regal manner and confident bearing. She came out to greet him personally and sent for the ministers, saying she had chosen her husband.

'You will have to perform three tasks to prove yourself suitable to rule over Mithila,' the ministers told Mahajanak.

Mahajanak was eager to regain his father's lost throne. And after meeting the princess, he was equally keen to win her hand as well. But he did not display any enthusiasm. He simply asked what the tasks were.

'First, you will have to identify the head of the princess's square bed,' the prime minister said.

Mahajanak sat down on the bed and thought for a while. Then he asked the princess for a hair pin and wanted to know where it should be placed. She pointed to a particular place. 'That is the head of the bed,' Mahajanak said right away. 'It is the place where the princess puts away her hair pins when she lies down at night.'

The princess was delighted and all the ministers were impressed with his wisdom. Next, an enormous bow was brought out that had a hundred men staggering under its weight.

'You will have to prove your strength by stringing this bow,' said the ministers.

Their eyes almost popped out when Mahajanak picked it up with the greatest of ease and strung it in a trice.

Now only the last test remained—to find the king's hidden treasure. Mahajanak asked for the clues.

'You will find the first pot where the sun rises, the second where it sets,' said the prime minister. In this manner, the minister gave Mahajanak the rest of the clues. Realising that something deeper lay behind the king's words, Mahajanak asked for some time to think about the problem. All night he tried to figure out the meaning of the clues.

The next day he asked, 'Did the king respect wise and learned men?' The prime minister looked at him curiously. 'He honoured them greatly,' he replied.

'Where did he receive them when they came to the palace?' Mahajanak asked next.

When the place was pointed out to him, he instructed them to dig there. Sure enough, the first pot of gold turned up.

'How did you guess?' asked the astonished ministers.

'It was the sun of wisdom that the king referred to in his clue,' Mahajanak said. 'Where did he bid farewell to them?'

The second pot of gold was recovered at this spot. In

this way, he managed to solve all the sixteen clues and unearthed the king's treasure.

The people of Mithila rejoiced that a suitable king had been found. But before his wedding and coronation could take place, Mahajanak insisted that his mother and his uncle, the kind Brahmin, be called from the city of Kalachampa.

When his mother arrived, he introduced her to the princess, saying, 'She was once the queen of Mithila.'

His mother blessed them saying, 'I knew you could do it, my son, I knew you would regain the lost throne of your father.'

Mahajanak married Shivali and was crowned king of Mithila. The first thing he did was to give away the sixteen pots of gold to the people of the land. Everyone blessed him for being a wise and generous ruler and predicted a long and happy reign for him.

The Snake Prince

A king called Surasra ruled over the city of Pratisthan. He had no children, which was a cause of great anxiety for him and his queen. After visiting many holy men and performing many rites, the queen became pregnant at last. But when the baby was born, to her horror, she found that she had given birth to a serpent!

They were facing a serious problem. How could they disclose that the prince of the country was a snake? The king and queen decided to conceal their son in a beautiful palace far from the city that only a few trusted servants would be allowed to enter. Thus they brought him up secretly. Whenever anyone asked, they would say that a holy man had advised them to keep the prince hidden from everyone's eyes. However, they constantly mourned the fact they had been cursed with such an unnatural child.

The serpent prince, whom they had named Nageshwar, could speak like a human. When he reached the appropriate age, he told the king, 'Dear father, it is time now that you performed my mundan and sacred thread ceremony. I would also like to study the Vedas, so please arrange for a teacher to instruct me. Unless one has studied the Vedas, one is not a complete person.'

The king was extremely upset at this request. How could these rituals be performed? And where would he find a teacher for a snake? But when his son insisted, he got a Brahmin to perform the ceremonies and also found a learned man who agreed to teach him the Vedas.

Surasra thought that his serpent son would be satisfied now. But one day, Nageshwar came up with another request. 'Dear father,' he said, 'I am of suitable age now. Please find me a bride.'

The king was utterly shocked. 'It pains me to say this, my son, but who will marry you?' he asked. 'No girl would like a snake for a husband.'

The serpent replied, 'There are many forms of marriage. And if you know how to go about it, you can arrange a match for me. Surely you can do this much for your son.'

The king returned to his palace, deep in thought. After discussing the matter with the queen, he decided to consult his ministers. 'The prince has now reached a marriageable age,' he said. 'He is a brave warrior, well-versed in all the arts. We have to find a suitable bride for him.'

The prime minister was a wise and venerable man. He said, 'In a country towards the east rules a king named Vijaya. He has eight sons and a daughter named Bhogwati. She is said to be a beautiful and intelligent girl. She would be a fit match for our prince.'

'Then there is no need for further delay,' said the king. 'Go and discuss the matter with King Vijaya.'

The prime minister travelled to King Vijaya's capital. The king was pleased with the proposal and accepted it. The wedding date was fixed and preparations began. But as the day drew near, Surasra became more and more anxious. How could he disclose in public that his son was a serpent? And would King Vijaya agree to go through with the wedding when he saw him?

The prime minister noticed that Surasra was becoming worried rather than joyful as the marriage date approached and being a wise man, he understood that there was a problem. He told the king, 'Do not worry, your majesty, I will take care of everything.'

The day of the wedding dawned and the marriage procession set out with elephants and horses and trumpets blowing. As he had promised, the prime minister took charge of everything. When they reached the bride's palace, he went to her father and said, 'Your majesty, as you are aware, the scriptures permit many forms of marriage. Unfortunately, due to unavoidable circumstances, Prince Nageshwar is unable to come personally. But we do not wish the auspicious time to pass without carrying out this important ceremony. If you have no objection, the rituals can be performed with the prince's sword as proxy.'

The king agreed and the princess was married to the sword. After a lavish celebration, she set off for her husband's home. According to custom, her old nurse also accompanied her.

At her new home, her father-in-law and mother-in-law received her lovingly. She was given a magnificent palace to live in, with all possible luxuries. To her surprise, however, there was no sign of her husband. The princess wondered why, but she decided to be patient, and wait. Sooner or later, she would have to meet the man whom she had married, she thought. She spent her time performing her duties towards her parents-in-law with great care. Soon, she had won their love and affection.

Nageshwar's palace was in a picturesque spot surrounded by flowering trees and shrubs, far away from the other palace buildings. Whenever his father and mother came to meet him, he would ask, 'When am I going to see my wife? Why doesn't she come to meet me?'

Finally, the queen realised that Bhogwati would have to learn the truth. She summoned her nurse and said, 'Your mistress must be keen to set eyes on her husband. But there is something you have to tell her. Prince Nageshwar is actually a snake and he is impatient to meet her.'

At first the old nurse was shocked at this deception and wept for her mistress. But after thinking over the matter, she came to the conclusion that no ordinary snake could be born to a human. She went to the princess and said, 'All this time we have been wondering why you have not met the prince. Today your mother-in-law told me the truth. You are extremely lucky, my child. You are married to a god who is a snake.'

Bhogwati was quite unperturbed. She simply said, 'I must surely have performed good deeds in my previous birth to get a god for a husband.'

The nurse conveyed Bhogwati's response to the king and queen. The king was moved to tears. 'We must have earned merit, too,' he told the queen, 'to be blessed with such a daughter-in-law.'

Then Bhogwati requested them to take her to her husband. She began to live in the palace with him and attended to his needs. One day Nageshwar asked her, 'People are afraid to look at my face, and because of that my parents have kept me in isolation. How is it that you are not frightened?'

'You are my husband. I love and respect you,' Bhogwati replied. 'Why should I be scared?'

Nageshwar's face brightened when she said this. And then he cried out in excitement, 'I remember now! Thanks to your love and devotion, I have regained my memory!' He took a deep breath. 'Do you know who I was in my previous birth? I was one of the serpents coiled around Shiva's arm. You were my wife, Bhogwati. One day Parvati cracked a joke and Shiva laughed. I could not help laughing too. The god was annoyed and cursed me to be born of a human. When I begged for mercy, he said, "Only when you worship me on the banks of the Gautami will you be freed from your curse."

Bhogwati was overjoyed. 'I knew you had to be someone special,' she exclaimed.

Nageshwar's parents were ecstatic to hear this too. Along with Bhogwati, the prince went to the banks of the river Gautami and worshipped Shiva. They were freed from the curse right away and assumed their divine forms. Now Nageshwar wanted to return to Shiva's service. But Surasra begged him to stay on. 'Please reign over my kingdom in my place,' he said, 'until you have children who can be your successors. Stay here at least till I am alive.'

Nageshwar agreed to his father's request. He ruled over the land wisely. When his father was no more, he appointed his own son in his place and went back to Shiva's abode. The place where he lived and ruled is known as Nagtirtha.

The Bell-Eared Demon

A village named Brahmapura was situated in the midst of thickly forested hills that were full of wild animals. It was a prosperous community, inhabited by simple and hardworking people.

One quiet afternoon, a thief crept towards the village temple, hoping to steal the offerings made there. But he found the doors locked and was unable to enter. The only thing he could find worth taking was the bell hanging outside. So he quietly removed that and ran away with it. He headed for the nearby hills, hoping to make his way to some other village where he could sell the bell. But as he was passing through the forest, a tiger leapt out and pounced on him. It killed the thief and ate him up.

The bell fell from the man's hand and lay there. Sometime later, a troop of monkeys came scampering by. They saw the bell and becoming curious about it, they picked it up. One of the monkeys had seen people ringing the bell at the temple when it had gone there looking for food. Imitating them, it took the bell and shook it hard. All the monkeys liked the sound and began to grab it from each other to ring it over and over again.

The sound of the bell echoed through the hills. Now it so happened that two travellers were passing that way. They found the dead thief's corpse lying on the hillside and just as they were wondering who could have killed the man, they heard the bell ring close by. Fearing for their lives, they fled from the spot as fast as they could. People were alarmed when they rushed into the village of Brahmapura, panting, and pale with fear.

'What's the matter?' they asked. 'Who are you running from? Why do you look so afraid?'

One of the travellers glanced over his shoulder fearfully. 'Some terrible creature lives up there in the hills,' he said. 'It has killed a man and devoured it.'

Just then the monkeys began to ring the bell. 'There! Can you hear it?' cried the second traveller. 'It makes that awful noise. Luckily we heard it coming and managed to escape with our lives!'

When they heard the sound, the villagers were also terror-struck. 'Suppose it comes into the village?' one asked with a shudder.

'Let us hope and pray it doesn't. We must never go up into the hills,' said another.

From that day onwards, everyone shivered and trembled whenever they heard the bell ring. All kinds of stories began to be made up about the terrible demon of the bell. Someone said it had huge ears that rang like bells whenever it moved about. They even named the demon Ghantakarna or Bell Ears.

Soon the fear of the bell-eared demon escalated to such a fever pitch that some of the villagers began to think of leaving the village. They went to the headman and said, 'We cannot live here anymore with this fearsome demon haunting this area. Any day it could come down to the village and devour us all.'

The headman got worried. If all the villagers ran away, there would be no village and no need for a headman. He would lose his importance. 'Have patience,' he told the villagers. 'A demon, however terrible, can be exorcised. Why do you want to leave your homes and go settle in a strange place? Your houses and your fields are all here; your ancestors have dwelt here for generations. I will find an exorcist to chase the demon away.'

A woman called Prabhavati also lived in the village. She was one of those rare beings who use their brains and are never influenced by superstitious talk. When she heard about the terrible demon of the bell, she refused to believe that such a creature existed. It's just the sound of a bell ringing, she thought. And unless I see the demon, I cannot believe there is such a creature. When she sat down and tried to puzzle out the mystery of the clanging bell, it suddenly struck her that the temple bell had vanished recently. Maybe some monkeys had taken it and were playing with it in the hills, she thought.

Then she heard that the headman was looking for someone to exorcise the demon. She went to him straightaway. 'I can get rid of the demon for you,' she said. 'But you will have to give me some money first.'

The people standing around began to laugh. 'You will chase away the demon that has struck fear into so many men's hearts?' they mocked. 'Don't be foolish. It will gobble you up right away.'

'Give me one chance,' Prabhavati said. 'After all, it's my life I'm risking, not yours.'

'She's right,' said the headman. 'Why not give her a chance?' He asked the village treasurer to give her some money.

Prabhavati went and bought some mangoes with the money. When they saw her, people laughed again. 'So, she is going to chase the demon away with mangoes!' one of the villagers mocked.

'Maybe it is a demon that is afraid of mangoes,' another scoffed.

Prabhavati ignored them. She went up to the hills with the mangoes tied in her sari pallu. She scattered them around and hid behind a tree. Let's see if the 'demon' comes out, she thought.

In no time at all, the monkeys smelt the mangoes. The whole troop arrived, leaping and prancing, and began to gobble them up. The monkey who was carrying the bell threw it down at once. They got so busy feasting on the mangoes that they did not notice that Prabhavati had picked up the bell.

Prabhavati returned to the village and went straight to the headman's house. 'I have brought the bell back,' she said, showing him the bell. 'Do you recognise it?'

'The temple bell!' cried the headman.

'Yes, that's what it is,' Prabhavati replied. 'Some monkeys had got hold of it and were playing with it.'

'You are truly a wise woman,' said the headman. 'The wisest among us.'

He rewarded her with much money. From that day on, everyone in Brahmapura respected Prabhavati for her wisdom. And the story of how she vanquished Ghantakarna, the demon of the bell, was told again and again.

Who Are My Real Children?

A man named Vasukarna lived in the city of Mathura. He was blessed with great wealth, but had no children to share it with. He and his wife constantly prayed for a child and conducted all kinds of rituals suggested by priests. Finally their devotion bore fruit and a son was born to them.

The delighted parents named the child Gokarna and according to custom, sent for an astrologer to cast his horoscope. The man foretold good fortune and added that he would have many children.

Gokarna grew up to be a devoted son. In due time, his parents got him married. But their hopes of having grandchildren stayed unfulfilled as Gokarna remained childless.

Recalling the astrologer's prediction, Gokarna consulted many holy men and performed all the rituals and good deeds they advised. One suggested that he construct a temple that was surrounded by five gardens full of flowers and fruit-bearing trees. Gokarna did so. The trees provided shade, shelter and fruit to birds and animals as well as to human beings. But, despite his sincere efforts, these good deeds produced no results.

Gokarna did not give up. Unfortunately, however, in his attempts to be blessed with offspring, he used up all his wealth in charitable deeds. And a time came when he had nothing left even to support his wife and parents.

Gokarna had no choice now but to try his luck in trade. Bidding farewell to his family, he set off with some companions to distant lands and was able to earn a reasonable amount of money. In the course of their travels, the group arrived at a beautiful valley. It was full of trees laden with luscious fruit. Tempted, the men hurried towards them and began to feast on the fruit.

There was no sign of anyone nearby, so they were astonished to hear a voice calling out, 'Please eat as much as you like.'

Like the others, Gokarna looked around to see who it could be. Then his eye fell on a parrot in a cage hanging from a tree, and realised with astonishment that it was speaking. 'It is written in the holy books that it is a sacred duty to honour a guest,' the bird continued.

'My parents are not here. When they arrive, they will offer you further hospitality.'

Amazed, Gokarna asked him if he really was a parrot or a divine being in this form.

'I was originally a disciple of the sage Vamadeva,' the parrot replied. 'And my name was Sukodara. Once, when the great sage Suka was performing penance, many learned sages approached him with questions about dharma. I too went there with my teacher. Eager to speak up, I kept interrupting. Irritated, Suka cursed me, saying, "This boy prattles like a parrot. Let him become one.'

'Immediately I turned into Suka or a parrot.

When the other sages begged him to have pity, Suka relented. 'I cannot take back my words,' he said, 'but he will be a very virtuous and learned parrot. He will achieve salvation in Mathura."

'Disconsolate, I flew away as far as I could and reached the Himalayas,' the parrot continued. 'But a hunter trapped me and put me in this cage.'

Gokarna was intrigued with his story. 'I come from Mathura,' he said. 'I will take you there so you can gain salvation.'

When the hunter and his wife returned, Gokarna pleaded with them to give him the parrot. 'I have no children,' he said. 'Let me keep him as my son.'

The hunter agreed on one condition. 'You must pass

on the merit one gains by bathing at the confluence of the Yamuna and Saraswati at Mathura to me,' he said.

Gokarna agreed. He returned to Mathura with Suka. The parrot lived happily in his home and they spent many pleasant hours discussing religion and morals. Then the day came when Gokarna once again found himself short of money. He decided to go and search for gems in the ocean and hired a ship for the purpose. Taking Suka with him, he set off.

While they were on their way, a fierce storm blew up. The ship was tossed so wildly by the waves that it seemed it would soon sink.

The terrified sailors cried out, 'There is a sinner on board who is responsible for our plight!'

Gokarna immediately felt guilty, because it was believed that a childless person cannot gain salvation. He said to Suka, 'My son, I'm afraid I might be the sinner. What should I do?'

Suka told him not to worry. 'I will go and find out,' he said.

Suka flew to a region in the north called Dhruva. Finally, he reached a huge mountain which had a beautiful temple of Vishnu on its peak. He flew around it, then went and hid inside. As he sat there, pondering over his problem, he saw many lovely goddesses covered with sweet-smelling flowers coming to worship at the temple.

Suka also noticed several Jatayu birds clustered on the

southern side of the temple. He decided to consult them. 'My father is in a storm-tossed ship and I have flown here to seek help. Can you save him?' he asked.

'We will surely help you,' the generous birds replied.

'I will split the waters with my feet and carry your father here on my back,' one of them offered.

The bird flew to the ship with Suka and carried Gokarna back. Gokarna immediately visited the temple and thanked the god for saving him.

After a while, the goddesses arrived. Hearing his tale, they gave him celestial fruit to eat. 'This will rid you of all your sorrows,' they said. 'You can stay here as long as you wish.'

Gokarna began to live there. In the meantime, the storm abated and a fair wind blew the sailors to a spot where they found many valuable gems. They collected a large quantity of them. But they felt sorry now that Gokarna had been forced to leave the ship and decided to pass on his share to his family.

By now Gokarna was getting anxious about his wife and parents. He told Suka, 'My family must be worrying about me. My friend, will you fly to Mathura please and inform my parents that I am safe and sound?'

'As you say,' Suka replied. 'If only I had been a larger bird, I could have carried you on my back. But at least I can go and reassure your parents.'

He winged off to Mathura right away. But Gokarna's

parents were not convinced that their son was still alive. They asked Suka to stay with them and tell them stories that might relieve their sorrow.

Then the sailors returned and gave Gokarna's share of gems to his parents. Grateful, the old couple treated them as honoured guests. In turn, the sailors began to take care of them as if they were their sons.

Gokarna continued to live near the temple, longing to get home somehow. Then he got an unpleasant surprise. When the goddesses arrived for their usual worship one day, he was shocked to find they had lost their limbs and become deformed.

'What reduced you to this state?' he asked, horrified.

'We live near a temple in Mathura,' the goddesses said sadly, 'surrounded by five beautiful gardens. We are the spirits of the trees that grow there. The king of Ayodhya came on a pilgrimage to Mathura and stayed in these gardens with his retinue. His soldiers cut down all the trees we live in. They destroyed all the flowers and fruits and only the trunks and roots were left. Along with the trees, our forms were also destroyed.'

'Is that so?' Gokarna asked, extremely agitated. 'Please tell me one thing, what merit does one gain by planting a garden?'

'The trees you plant are like your children,' the goddesses replied. 'They provide flowers and fruit and shade to the weary. Birds live in their branches, so do many animals. Planting trees is like giving birth to children.'

When he heard these words, Gokarna fainted right away. The goddesses hurriedly revived him. 'Alas,' he cried, 'I am the owner of the gardens you mention. If I had been there, I would not have let this happen. I spent much money to gain offspring—without success. Little did I know that the trees were my children! If only I could return home! I would tell the king what has happened to you.'

'We can take you there easily,' said the goddesses. They seated him on an aerial chariot and flew to Mathura, carrying a large quantity of gems and wondrous fruits. When he reached home, Gokarna immediately went to the king with his gifts. He told him how the destruction of the trees had harmed the goddesses, and begged him to restore the gardens.

The king immediately gave orders that the gardens be brought back to their original condition. In time, the trees revived and the goddesses regained their former beauty. Having learned what a good deed it is to plant a garden, the king created several in his city and instructed his citizens to do so too.

Gokarna planted many more gardens as well, happy to believe that the plants and trees were his children. Full of gratitude towards Suka, he built a temple too, where the learned parrot began to live.

Suka died there and went straight to heaven.

Animals Are More Grateful

A man set out from his village to visit a distant town. His way lay through a dense forest. It was a hot day and after he had tramped for a while, he got thirsty. After a long search, he came across a well.

But when he bent to draw water, he got a shock. The well was a dry one and loud voices were coming from it. Soon he discovered that a lion, a snake, a goldsmith and a barber had fallen into it. All of them begged him to help them out.

'Please save me, O noble human,' called the lion. 'I'll be grateful to you for the rest of my life.'

'Never!' the traveller shook his head hard. 'You're a ferocious beast and will gobble me up the moment I pull you out.'

'I'm not so ungrateful,' said the lion. 'I promise, I won't touch a single hair on your head.'

The man felt sorry for the lion. He looked around and found some strong creepers and lowered them into the well.

'Here, hold these tight,' he said. He tugged and heaved and finally managed to pull the lion out.

The lion bowed to him and said, 'How can I thank you? If you pass this way again, please come and visit me so I can repay your good deed. But before I go, I'll give you some advice. Don't take those two men out of the well.'

The man was puzzled, but he heard the snake calling out, 'Save me! Please save me!'

'Not on my life,' said the traveller. 'I can't take chances with a poisonous creature like you.'

'Do you really think I can be so thankless?' asked the snake. 'You took a chance with the lion. I beg you, have faith in me too.'

Again, the man's heart melted and he helped the snake out of the well. Before it left, the snake said, 'If ever you are in trouble, just think of me. I'll come to your help immediately. But I'd like to do you a good turn before I go. Don't take those two men out. You'll regret it.'

However, the barber and the goldsmith began to shout from inside the well. 'Help! Help! You rescued two dangerous beasts,' they cried. 'Will you abandon your fellow men and go away?'

The man thought, how can they harm me? I'll never be able to forgive myself if I leave them here to die.

So he lowered the creepers into the well again and pulled the men out one by one. They too thanked him, saying, 'We live in the big city nearby. You must visit us so we can reward you for saving our lives.'

The man reached his destination, completed his work and set out for the return journey to his village. As he passed through the forest again, he remembered what the lion had said, and decided to visit him.

'Welcome, my good friend,' said the lion. 'I'm delighted to see you again. I've been saving a little gift for you, just in case you came to visit me. Please accept this diamond ring.'

'A diamond ring?' asked the man, astonished to get such a gift from a lion. 'Thank you very much.' He slipped the ring on his finger.

When it was time for him to go, the lion said again, 'If you're ever in trouble, remember, I'm always there to help you.'

Now the city where the goldsmith and barber lived fell in the man's way, so he decided to visit them as well. He wanted to sell the diamond ring and hoped the goldsmith could help him get a good price.

He found the goldsmith's house quite easily. He seemed to be well-known in the city.

'Welcome, my benefactor,' said the goldsmith, bowing low. 'How can I forget what you did for me? I must send for the barber. We often think about you. Do you know? He's an important man now, the chief of the king's police.'

Soon the barber arrived and two of them entertained their benefactor well, with the daintiest of dishes and their company.

'What can I do for you?' asked the goldsmith. 'You saved our lives. Any favour you ask would be small compared to what you did for us.'

'Well said, my friend,' said the barber. 'Please let me know too if you need anything. I'd do anything to help you.'

'That's very kind of you,' the helpful man replied. 'There is indeed something. I just visited the lion and he gave me a gift of a fine diamond ring. But what use is a diamond ring to a poor man like me? If you could help me to sell it, I would be very grateful.' And he showed them the ring.

The goldsmith examined the ring carefully. 'It is very valuable indeed,' he said. 'Far more valuable than you could ever imagine. Of course, I will help you, my friend.'

He turned to the barber and said, 'Friend, I know it is time to go and attend to your duties. I will walk with you till the gate, while our benefactor rests here after his journey.'

The barber said goodbye and the two of them set off while the good man relaxed, pleased to find such a comfortable place to spend the night.

Now, the goldsmith had recognised the ring because he himself had made it for the princess of the land. It so happened that a wild animal had killed this princess while she was travelling through the forest. All her attendants fled and saved their lives. They did not dare return and tell her father because they would be punished. When there was no news, the king announced that whoever provided any information about her would receive a big reward.

'This is a great opportunity,' the goldsmith whispered to the barber. 'We should turn this man in.' The barber agreed at once.

The two hurried to the palace and told the king that they had found the man who had murdered the princess. The king ordered the barber to arrest him and throw him in prison. When he found the ring on the good man's finger, he was convinced that he had killed his daughter.

The good man swore he was innocent, but no one believed him. They could not believe that a lion could present a man with a ring! He was sentenced to death right away.

As he sat in his cell, waiting to be hanged, he thought, sighing, how I wish I had followed the advice of the snake and the lion! Oh, why did I save these two ungrateful men from the well?

To his astonishment, the snake appeared, saying, 'Did you think of me, friend? What can I do to help you?'

'Dear friend, if it is within your powers to save me

from death, please help me!' cried the man. He told the snake all that had happened.

'I told you not to save those two wicked fellows,' said the snake. 'But it's no use saying that now. Of course I will help you. There is one way. I'll go and bite the queen. When they're searching for a cure, you should send word to the king that you know how to treat a snake bite. I'll come and remove the poison from her body again and the king will pardon you.'

'How can I thank you?' cried the man.

The same night, the snake crept into the queen's room and bit her while she slept. She screamed in pain, all her maids came running and discovered what had happened. The king sent for all the doctors and healers in the kingdom right away. But none of them could do anything for the queen. Her condition became worse and worse and the king was in despair.

The next morning, the jailer came to take the good man to be hanged. When he was asked what his last wish was, he said he would like to save the queen's life. No one believed him at first. However, the king felt that a man who was about to die would not make false claims and his last wish should be honoured. The good man was taken to the palace and the moment he entered, he thought of his friend, the snake. The snake crept in and sucked out the poison from the queen's body. Immediately she sat up, hale and hearty again.

The king said, 'I thank you for saving the queen's life, but I cannot forgive you for killing my daughter.'

'I did not kill her,' cried the good man. 'Please ask the barber and the goldsmith how I pulled them out from a well, along with the snake and the lion. It was the lion who gave me the ring.'

The barber and the goldsmith were called, but they denied it all. 'We were never inside a well, your majesty,' they said. 'And we've never set eyes on this man before we found him with the princess's ring.'

'Ah, the lion and snake were right when they said that I should leave these two men in the well,' the good man cried. 'If only the lion could come and bear witness that I'm speaking the truth!

'A lion as a witness!' scoffed the barber and the goldsmith. 'He really knows how to make up stories. Your majesty, he is only putting off the moment of his death.'

They had barely finished speaking when a loud roar startled everyone. The king's attendants ran to look out of the window. A huge lion stood outside!

'This is astonishing beyond belief,' said the king. 'There is no doubt that this man is speaking the truth. It seems animals are more grateful than men.'

He ordered the goldsmith and the barber to be thrown into prison immediately. The good man was rewarded with a purse of gold coins and returned to his village, relieved and happy.